I0676833

Highland Guardian: One True Love

by

Dee Corcoran

Copyright Notice
This is a work of fiction. Names, characters, places, and incidents are either the product of the author's imagination or are used fictitiously, and any resemblance to actual persons living or dead, business establishments, events, or locales, is entirely coincidental.

Highland Guardian: One True Love

COPYRIGHT © 2023 by Dee Corcoran

All rights reserved. No part of this book may be used or reproduced in any manner whatsoever without written permission of the author or The Wild Rose Press, Inc. except in the case of brief quotations embodied in critical articles or reviews.
Contact Information: info@thewildrosepress.com

Cover Art by *The Wild Rose Press, Inc.*

The Wild Rose Press, Inc.
PO Box 708
Adams Basin, NY 14410-0708
Visit us at www.thewildrosepress.com

Publishing History
First Edition, 2024
Trade Paperback ISBN 978-1-5092-5476-7
Digital ISBN 978-1-5092-5475-0

Published in the United States of America

Dedication

Dedicated to my parents, Ruth Welch and Alan
Corcoran. Thank you so very much, Lynn, Pam,
Joanne, Kevin, and Alan, for your encouragement and
belief in me.

Chapter 1

February 15, 1692. Coire Gabhail, Glencoe, Scotland.

The call of thunder sent Kayleigh MacDonald to the mouth of the cave. She went outside, bow in hand, quiver strapped to her shoulder. Protected from the cold with three layers of breeches and sweaters, she ran along the ledge behind the brush. She stood, bow and arrow nocked, waiting for an intruder. Her thighs ached, stomach complained. She rolled her shoulders to sooth the stiffness in her neck.

The darkness of morning in the predawn cold would soon be lit by a brightening sky, the best time to catch movement leaving the shelter of trees to travel the flat surface at the bottom. Kayleigh scanned the length of the valley, lingering on areas where men could hide. Up and down the valley walls, left to right, then across the bottom. It would be easy to warm among the cattle huddled there, where eyes couldn't see and sound wouldn't escape the herd. She hoped no one found the valley. Only MacDonalds, famous for hiding cattle in the middle of nowhere, knew the location. Coire Gabhail belonged to them.

The last roll of thunder had been two days ago, the thunder of battle, of redcoats firing on her home and the homes of all now hiding in the cave she guarded. The

Campbells attacking Glencoe had not located *Coire Gabhail*, and some of the MacDonalds knew its location.

Ice blue. It interrupted her train of thought. *Blue? Light. On the snow. Now it's gone. Human presence in Deer Cave. He would be forced to move over the path between the boulders.* She reached for the pile of rocks by the cave entrance and released the twine, which lowered the weighted flag inside the cave. Alerted to danger, silence followed. She hadn't noticed the low hum of activity in the cave until it ceased. Now, she heard footsteps on the path. Stealth. Someone approached with extreme care.

She waited at the end of the path, bow drawn. A crash, cursing, and metal clattered on the rocks. A sword? Adrenaline surged through her, increasing her strength and precision. She set her aim. Warmth and a whisper of movement behind her hinted at her sister Brighde's presence. Kayleigh drew and held her breath, ready to release the arrow with a second to follow.

A face appeared, then shoulders. She released the arrows.

"Aiden!" Brighde warned him in time for him to turn back. One arrow just missed his head, instead striking the rock wall behind him. The other snagged his hood. Except for his face, he was covered in dried blood.

"Not mine, the blood," Aiden said, last seen before the attack three days ago.

"Oh, thank goodness," Kayleigh said.

Brighde worked the arrow out of his hood.

"Washed my face and arms with snow."

She peeked inside the cave. "Debra, a clean cloak for Aiden, please."

Aiden, wearing the new cloak, entered the cave.

Brighde rearranged the cave curtain and reset the flag. Their cousin Debra took watch outside.

The MacDonald women and children inside the cave looked over at them, hopeful faces awaiting news of their men.

Kayleigh turned to Aiden. "What did you drop?"

"A climbing spike fell. I'll be leaving soon."

"You're leaving?" she said.

"I came to bring the extra climbing equipment. And to check on you women. Don't worry. The fighting was over on the thirteenth. Last redcoat left yesterday. You still have the smell of smoke here."

"Part of it comes from our hearth fire." Kayleigh's Aunt Ilsa handed him a cup of warmed whiskey.

"Thank you." He took a long drink and another. "We're tracking the men. Callan reports most have joined the search. Glencoe was destroyed by fire. Most of the men are off making living arrangements for their families."

"I had to gather strength to report…it isn't good news," he said.

"How many?" said Kayleigh.

"Thirty-eight, including Mac. Women and children too. Mairi, he passed in my arms with your name on his lips."

Oh no. Kayleigh found Mairi's face in the group and averted her eyes. Mairi had already drawn herself together and held her head high, a mark of Scottish stoicism, a posture intended to comfort others when a woman wanted to wail her loss. Her quivering chin gave evidence of the pain inside.

"She doesn't even have his child to comfort her," Brighde whispered her heartfelt observation.

"We'll care for her. The women have grown together here at Coire Gabhail," Kayleigh said.

Ilsa traded a bowl of stew for his empty cup.

He ate the stew and returned the bowl to her. "Thanks to you," he said.

Kayleigh hugged him.

"It's time to leave." He stepped back and looked into her eyes. "I need to go."

Brighde had been preparing a package for him containing bandages, ointment, and clean clothes, all wrapped in blankets. "If there is no need now, just leave them in Deer Cave."

"I will. Deer Cave?"

"We took a vote and named the caves," Kayleigh said.

"I see. And this one?"

"Clan Cave."

"Good name."

She added two flasks of ale to his bundle. "Mind you, don't drop these."

"On my life. I will hold them close."

"We've been saving those for you and the men. We also have the whiskey from Caledonia."

"Caledonia. The thought brings a smidgen of peace. Green grasses and flowers. Abundance. No blizzards. A sprinkling of snow each winter. It has all but passed this year. We're heading into Spring and already have bluebells."

Ilsa had joined them. "How can this be? It's midwinter here. Is it far to Caledonia?"

"It's closer than you would think," Aiden said. "A couple of hours' journey. You'll see."

"I hope to visit one day," said Ilsa.

"Me too," said Kayleigh. "In all these years, I haven't been there."

"When touched by Caledonia, you want to stay forever," he said. "Now, I must head to Glencoe to help arrange things."

"Be safe," said Brighde.

Kayleigh took two more flasks of ale and followed him to Deer Cave, still carrying her bow.

She helped store the supplies at Deer Cave and insisted Aiden drink ale before he left. He put dried food in his pack and rolled two blankets to carry on his back, flasks at his waist. His brother Callan and Debra's husband Raibert would be by to gather more supplies.

"Thanks to you," he said.

She smiled and reached to cup his face and kiss him. He held the kiss a moment longer as he held her close. He insisted on seeing her off to Clan Cave before he left, and she hugged him with all his supplies. Tilting her head, she left him with a smile.

****

She pulled aside the Clan Cave curtain to see everyone covered with MacDonald plaids, creating a sea of comfort. The clan tartan had proved to be the possession most revered. Everyone had a plaid for protection and wore more than one set of clothing. All hid in the cave prior to the attack.

The women and children in the cave awaited news of the men who had obeyed the warning of the impending attack, getting the women and children to the safety of Coire Gabhail.

Each person slept under a plaid or two, protected from the cold deep in the cave. The children slept farthest back in the cave, their mothers positioned between them and danger, armed with sharp blades. The older women were with them. The single women of childbearing age sat between the mothers and the cave opening, an even more dangerous area, holding blades and spears. Aunt Ilsa had insisted on guarding the mothers with the single women, though she was past child-bearing age. She refused to be considered an elder. They slept with at least two on watch in four-hour shifts, night and day.

Kayleigh's watch lasted throughout the night, with a short shift at midday. Brighde and Debra shared watch with her. The watch inside slept between the women and the mouth of the cave—never a restful position, much less in the cold of midwinter. The hearth fire near the center of the cave kept drafts from reaching the back and helped keep the front from freezing temperatures.

****

Kayleigh grew fearful. It had been a full two days since Aiden had visited. He should have returned in the night unless a threat remained. A more honorable man didn't exist. He would never abandon those in his charge. The alternative was he'd been wounded...or killed. Fear stabbed her heart. Even her bones ached with the thought.

The children slept in a makeshift room with the older girls. Stacks of blankets, tartans, and clothing divided the rear half of the cave into two rooms. The older boys slept outside this area, considering themselves the rear guard. They formed a final line of defense between the enemy and the women.

Kayleigh returned inside, with Debra and Brighde outside. The Deer Cave was farther back along the cliff. The third cave was attached inside the Clan Cave, holding stored food, ale, and whiskey. Though the hearth fire warmed Clan Cave, it didn't reach far into the stores. Kayleigh looked around at the women. Stress showed while looking after one another or when hearing an unexpected noise. She hoped her own face masked the fear in her gut. Over their heads, her eyes met Brighde's. The men should have arrived by now.

Squirrels looking for warmth entertained the children. They fed the squirrels acorns, and food scraped from the bottoms of the cooking pots. Their antics were welcomed as a distraction, yet the noise they made entering the cave was always unexpected.

****

In the night, the women went to the mouth of the cave where Kayleigh stood outside looking at the ethereal white disk one-quarter the size of Coire Gabhail. Snow on the ground appeared liquid silver. Shadowed eyes regained brightness as varying degrees of hope bloomed on uplifted faces. Postures relaxed for a moment. Whispers of encouragement fluttered in the breeze like hummingbird wings. Smiles shimmered. Kayleigh stepped inside to absorb the radiating warmth. Water boiled, oats cooked, a pot of honey heated by the fire, and the women worked together to make it all happen.

Brighde handed her a cup of warmed whiskey.

"Thank you. Go outside and see the moon. It's stunning." She brought the cup close to her face. Soon, her skin felt supple, no longer frozen. Courage in the face of fear had taken its toll.

Not having heard news of the men, the returning women's faces still bore their stress. Physical comfort and emotional state were close cousins. What happened to one always affected the other. The more she learned about these women, she grew to love them. From this day forward, they would forever be connected, twenty close cousins indeed. Beautiful, inside and out. She looked around at all the women and wondered who else might suffer loss. They hid worries from the children. As long as they tended to one another, they held it together. With the women awake, naked fear showed when a noise interrupted their thoughts.

Aiden's brother Callan entered the cave with Brighde close behind him.

"I found him sleeping on his way here. He sent pebbles scattering," she said.

"Not sleeping. I leaned against the wall for a moment."

Callan stood before Kayleigh. He hadn't mentioned Aiden.

"Where is he?"

Cold fear invaded her. She went still. Brighde joined them. Wanting to scream, Kayleigh remembered Mairi's stoic stance and instead squared her shoulders.

"Aiden?" Kayleigh's voice struggled past her thickened throat.

She braced herself.

Chapter 2

"We have no report regarding Aiden. I'm sure he will return." Callan paled as he spoke about his brother.

She could see he was sure of no such thing. Her heart ripped, opening an abyss of pain.

Brighde pulled her into a hug. Kayleigh sobbed without sound, tears falling onto her shoulder. Callan's large body behind them blocked the view for the sake of privacy.

When she breathed again without sniffles, she worried for him and Brighde. They loved Aiden as much as she did. Aiden also had acted as a brother to Brighde her entire life. Brighde's face even now held traces of tears. She embraced them in a small group hug of mutual support.

Callan held both women, one on each side. "I cannot wait here. Someone knows what happened to him. He could lie outside the tunnel, perhaps too weak to stand, and be waiting for me to find him. I must go."

"I'll go with you." Kayleigh would rather be active in searching. The thought of staying there waiting made her want to scream.

"No. The women need you. Brighde will remain with you."

Brighde handed him a flask of warm whiskey. "Go with God." Her thought gave Kayleigh a sliver of hope. The tiny ray shed light on her soul.

The women tended to Mairi, whose tears flowed down her face. There was no hope for her husband. At least Kayleigh had renewed hope with the possibility of Aiden's return.

****

Kayleigh opened the covering so Brighde could guide Raibert into the cave. He had returned with news and was wearing a clean plaid. She heard the relief in Debra's fervent greeting and his mumbles of reassurance. They had been married only a few months. An exchange of questions and answers followed, but she couldn't make out the words.

Brighde came back out, arms loaded with supplies. "He saw Aiden last night. Swears he lives."

Kayleigh helped with her load. "He did promise to return. Aiden's honorable, keeps his promises. He's never broken his word."

The sisters shared silence for a time, keeping watch outdoors together and finding peace in the mere presence of each other.

"I can't stay here. I'll wait outside the tunnel," Brighde said.

"No. There is no shelter, no safety. I will not allow you to go."

"I meant I would wait in the cave on this side of the tunnel."

"You may need more bandages and whiskey. Set the blankets to hang over the cave entrance. Cover both entrances to contain the fire's heat. It will warm faster. I will join you in waiting," Kayleigh said.

"Thank you."

"Debra and Raibert will keep watch."

****

They gathered the supplies and set off to Deer Cave.

Hearing steps behind her, Kayleigh thought it must be Debra needing something. Instead, Fiona followed her, and without the necessary clothing to protect her from the cold.

"Fiona, go back to the cave."

"You're not my boss."

"Yes, I am. Aiden left me in charge. You heard him yourself when he left us here."

"He left you in charge of the cave, not of me, since I'm outside the cave."

"He left me in charge of the lives of everyone in the cave. He left me responsible for your life. Now stop quibbling like a child and go where you belong."

"I want to welcome him when he returns. He'll need a warm body to cuddle with. Your frozen self isn't woman enough for him."

"He won't be in the mood, Fiona."

"You want Aiden for yourself."

"Get your arse back in the cave before I pick up your tiny self and put it there. If I need to do this, then I will tie your hands and feet. You will be humiliated."

"Hmph." Fiona turned back and entered the cave.

"Let us proceed, dear sister," Brighde said.

"I don't feel very dear right now."

"Would you have tied her?" Brighde asked with a smile.

"Yes. On second thought, maybe as a last resort."

When they reached Deer Cave, Brighde stored the supplies, and Kayleigh started a fire using flint and wood stored in the cave.

Together, they built and stoked the fire. A pot of snow was set to melt with a smaller pot of whiskey near it. A pot of Ilsa's stew would be next.

They hung blankets over the tunnel and valley entrances to the cave to block the draft.

After darkness had fallen, they relaxed with a long drink, each resting against a pile of plaids.

"Our men will return," Brighde nodded.

"Brighde, how can you be so certain?" Kayleigh took a long drink.

"Faith. We are meant to be together."

"Then why haven't you married?"

"Callan has not asked. Not since our childhood. After he grows, and his eyes follow only me, I will allow him to ask again." She ladled another cupful for each of them. "Aiden grew to adulthood when he was young. You should consider marrying him."

"I'll remind you I am handfasted. He may not be here, but the contract is real. Besides, Aiden would have to ask me, and I don't see it happening. Then I would have to say no."

****

They arrived noisy and covered in blood.

Alerted by the men's voices echoing through the tunnel, Kayleigh and Brighde had warmed whiskey ready for them.

"The blood belongs to dead MacDonalds," Aiden reported. "They died in our arms on the thirteenth after the attack. Men, women, and children. It was just before dawn, they were dressed in nightclothes. One woman didn't use the tartan she carried. It could have prevented her death. They were terror-stricken. By the fourteenth, we found them frozen to death, having tried to escape the militia."

"Such a waste. It'll be weeks before they can have a

proper Christian burial. They are in the high caves of Coire Gabhail." Callan drained his cup in one gulp.

Brighde asked, "How did you do it without us hearing it?"

"It was during the howling wind on the fourteenth. The high caves are at the far end, away from the cave the women are using." Callan reached for the second cup of warm whiskey Brighde handed him, as Kayleigh did for Aiden.

After a long drink, Aiden picked up a clean cloth, dipped it into the pot of hot water, and wiped his face. Shadows of grief clouded his blue eyes. When they met Kayleigh's, they gentled.

"They froze on the hillside, trying to escape. It is damned hard to bury good people." Callan's voice thickened, and he stopped speaking. Brighde wiped his face.

Aiden stretched and stared at the ceiling. "And the women and children." His arms dropped when he could speak again, his straight shoulders curved downward. "It was brutal, cruel." His voice shook. "A new level of cruelty in the Highlands."

Kayleigh wiped his face and neck until clean and again to soothe him.

"We'll see you later," said Brighde. She and Callan returned to Clan Cave.

Kayleigh turned away as Aiden removed his kilt, and then she helped by washing his back. She tried to look away, but images of Aiden nude were etched into her brain. She shivered from awareness. He was beautiful. She had brought fresh clothing for him.

"Burn the soiled clothing," he said.

"Later," she said.

Warmed whiskey helped with the pain of body and mind. Not one drop of all the blood had been his. He had held friends as they bled out onto the snow.

She sat blanketed with his head in her lap as he slept, dressed and covered with blankets. She stroked his hair to calm him, then lay beside him. His long lashes gave the appearance of innocence. He turned to lean into her, head on her shoulder and one arm around her, giving comfort. His face was so close she could kiss him.

"Go ahead and do it," he said.

She looked at him to see blue glinting through half-closed eyes. She met his challenge by rubbing her lips on his. His hand cupped the back of her head to extend and deepen the kiss. He ended with two tender kisses.

"Good sleep, love," he said.

"Good sleep, Aiden."

She cuddled with him. He rested his right hand on her back beneath the plaid.

****

"You need to come with us to Caledonia," Aiden said.

"Absolutely not," Kayleigh said, raising her chin. "I plan to go home to Glencoe."

"Your home is in no condition for living."

"I can rebuild."

"There's nothing to rebuild."

"Even so, I want to see for myself."

"I want to spare you the pain of viewing the loss. They set fire to the village. It is gone."

"No. It can't be. Mother's quilt. Brighde's books. Mairi's needlework. My bow and arrow collection. My first bow, the one you carved for me. Robbie..." Kayleigh's eyes filled, and tears dropped.

"I saved Robbie the rascal cat and a few other things. You need to find a way to let go of the desire to return home. There is no home. It would cause even more pain for you to see the devastation."

"Must you be so direct?"

"You like me being direct. It's part of my charm." His smile didn't reach his eyes. "I understand feeling overwhelmed. Suffice it to say I did what I could to alleviate your loss before the attack. I brought Robbie the cat and your things to Caledonia, Brighde's, and Ilsa's too. You see, I believed Will Campbell when he told us of the impending attack."

"Thank you."

"Do you agree to go to Caledonia with us? Graeme is waiting for us."

"What about Brighde, Aunt Ilsa, and Debra?"

"Raibert and Debra will go to her cousin's home. You know Brighde and Ilsa will follow your decision." He sighed. "And Fiona will follow me as she does."

"She will follow the women. You always said there are no blizzards in Caledonia."

"It's a magical place with green grass and fruit trees. We're having an early spring now."

"Fruit. Do you have pears?"

"Yes, we do."

"Is it where you got the—"

"Yes, the pear I gave you. I should have brought you more."

"I will have a pear when we reach Caledonia."

Aiden reached out to hold her hand. She shook his hand off and moved in front to lead them to the Glencoe tunnel.

****

Aiden groaned.

"Didn't I just say I wouldn't take you to Glencoe?"

"I'm taking myself to Glencoe."

"You can't return without me unlocking the tunnel entrance."

"You won't let it happen to me."

"Such faith."

"It's true, though, isn't it?"

"Yes. It's a good thing we brought weapons. Do you have daggers or only the bow?"

"I have them, as do you, and it's a good thing I wear trews," said Kayleigh.

"You'll be comfortable in Caledonia. The weather is warmer on the other side of the portal. The air is humid from the river, with wildflowers and weeping willows. Chestnuts, hazelnuts, pears, apples, and berries. Rose makes the best apple fritters and turnovers. I can't wait to show it all to you."

"We're nearing the silence level," he said.

"Okay," she whispered.

"Torches are extinguished here. And silence follows."

She nodded her agreement.

There were reasons the Campbells hadn't located Coire Gabhail.

They tread with a slow, silent pace from then on.

When they reached the portal, Kayleigh stepped back and averted her eyes. Aiden, Callan, Raibert, and a few others knew the motions to open the portal. Anyone entering or leaving Coire Gabhail vowed not to reveal any information regarding the journey and the portals. The vow was part of the MacDonald loyalty oath. Most entering wore blindfolds before the portals were reached in Glencoe. The cattle reivers knew of the other portal used to hide the cattle when Campbells were chasing them.

As she stepped forward into Glencoe, she hoped Aiden had exaggerated, though he was not prone to doing so.

She followed him around one of the three mountains called the sisters.

And stopped in horror. The village had been reduced to charred remains. All buildings had been razed with complete destruction. Not one building had been spared. There was nothing to go home to.

She stood in shock. Her heart pounded, eyes burned. Aiden turned her toward him and embraced her. She cried silent screams against his cloak. It was a living nightmare she would never forget.

Who would do this? King William? One of his men? How could anyone be so cruel? A few cows had been stolen over the years. The Campbells could afford the loss. MacDonalds had been hungry. Children needed milk and cheese and occasional meat to survive. Oats only went so far. It quieted tummies and made a good start to the day, but using it for all meals...that's when they needed to reive to survive. The Campbells wouldn't trade with them. Raibert and Aiden said Caledonia held abundance in food, in beauty, in good weather. Aunt Ilsa and Brighde would thrive there. Healing would be hard enough. There simply was nowhere else to go.

"Are you okay?" Aiden asked, his hands squeezing her shoulders.

"I will be." She sighed and shuddered. "You are right. We'll go to Caledonia," she said.

"I know you resign yourself to the inevitable.

Graeme already approved the request to move you, Brighde, Ilsa, Mairi, and Fiona to Caledonia. It's my home. I hope you grow to love it as I do. Do you need one final look?"

"No."

He stroked her hair, and when she looked at him, he wiped snowflakes off her cheeks.

He stepped around her to guide her back to the portal.

"This helped you decide."

"Yes. Thank you for bringing me."

After lighting the torches from the wall candle, which Kayleigh snuffed out, their return to Deer Cave was quick.

Brighde had returned to clean. The cave looked as it had when they arrived the day prior. They returned to Clan Cave.

Brighde grabbed Kayleigh and hugged her tight. "Your eyes are red with lavender circles beneath them. You saw it?"

Aiden stood behind her, hands resting on her shoulders in support.

"Yes. It wasn't an exaggeration. All is gone. And it doesn't begin to describe it." Her voice cracked, and her eyes teared as she spoke.

"Such cruelty. I never knew," said Brighde.

Callan turned her into his arms.

Ilsa and Debra brought them bracing cups of whisky and cups of oatmeal with honey.

"No guarding for you tonight," said Debra. "Callan and Raibert will take the night watch."

****

Two days later, the men had made several trips

reuniting families who had been separated in their flight from Glencoe. Debra and Raibert joined another family traveling to Edinburgh. Families went to America or France, or to family elsewhere in Scotland. Others were sheltered and protected by clans outraged by the atrocity done to the MacDonalds. They carried their plaids, rations, and flasks of ale. They also took any treasures they had brought with them to Coire Gabhail. Each family had enough to arrive at their destination.

Kayleigh, Brighde, Ilsa, Mairi, and Fiona would travel with Aiden and Callan to Caledonia, the place where the men had been raised with Graeme, their older brother and Chief of their MacDonald clan.

"Pack light. Carry what is necessary, nothing more." Kayleigh wanted to be sure Mairi and Ilsa didn't have too much to carry. Brighde pulled back Kayleigh's cinnamon-colored hair and tied it using a strip of tartan.

Callan and Brighde filled and moved bins to restore order in the cave. It looked as it had before the events in Glencoe, except though they had swept, a large burned area marked the floor of Clan Cave. It had held the hearth. The embers had warmed the ache of tired bodies and the emotional exhaustion of women and children without homes in winter. It had nurtured them with sustenance. Pots of soup, water, whiskey, and porridge. Oats had filled empty stomachs, as always. Kayleigh had gained a new appreciation for oatmeal.

Preparations complete, they set out for Caledonia.
****

They took a short flight of stairs in the back of cave three, the stores room. The tunnel was wide and tall enough for Aiden to stand straight. Farther into the tunnel, an older tunnel branched out to the valley. It had three sides, with the open side facing the deep valley of Coire Gabhail. It looked out at the tops of trees and several osprey nests.

"Mairi!" At Brighde's yell, Kayleigh dropped her pack to the path. Mairi had begun sliding down the side of the mountain. Brighde held her by the wrists, but Mairi slumped. Kayleigh helped Brighde pull her up. Ilsa stood by to help.

When Kayleigh stood on the path, it broke off, and she began falling. Callan reached for her, but she couldn't catch his hand. She found a foothold and lay flat against the mountain. She held onto an unstable bush with one hand, but her legs held the bulk of her weight. *How will I get back to the path? I'm larger than Mairi and weigh more.*

"Kayleigh! Kayleigh!" Fiona said as she stood there watching.

"Stop your wailing and do something. Get out of the way. Move farther along the path," Callan demanded.

Kayleigh's attention returned to her situation where she was facing the mountain. Aiden slammed into her, pinning her against the mountain. He seemed to stand on a ledge a little below her feet.

"Hold on to the mountain. Fasten your body to it," he said.

"Okay," she said.

Aiden had started a spike and rope for Mairi, who hadn't needed it because Brighde and Kayleigh had rescued her. Callan tied off the rope and threw it to them.

"You are safe," Aiden said.

"You're sure?" Kayleigh said.

"With me, Aiden."

His breath warmed her nape. "Yes," she whispered.

"Say it."

"I am safe."

"With Aiden."

"Yes."

"Always. Safe with me." He leaned his head against her back. "I love you."

In grave danger on the side of a mountain, Kayleigh's world righted itself. He loved her.

Aiden fastened the rope around her waist and legs. She wasn't a climber, but her fitness level allowed her to climb as those above rescued her. Aiden waited until she was lifted out of reach before he climbed the mountain back to the solid wall of the path, where he helped Callan and Brighde raise her. It was slow going, one secure step at a time. At the top, Aiden was there to grab her and pull. She had scraped her face and torn her trews. He held her close and then guided her to the secure Caledonian side of the path.

"I should have foreseen this," Callan shook his head. "Mairi is worn out."

"Poor lass just gave out," Ilsa said as she stroked Mairi's back.

"Fiona tried to squeeze past Mairi and bumped into her," Brighde said. "I saw the whole thing."

"I was trying to get next to Aiden where it's warmer." Fiona's hands were clenched into fists at her side. "I didn't mean to hurt her."

"You may be small, but I didn't know you were small-minded," Brighde said. "You are irresponsible. Stay behind Callan. You're a danger to us. Kayleigh could still tie you and leave you out here to freeze."

Before they left, Aiden and Callan used spikes and rope to cordon off the dangerous part of the path.

Kayleigh walked behind Fiona, with Brighde behind Kayleigh. Callan led this time with Aiden at the rear carrying Mairi in his arms.

Chapter 3

She should have expected it. Aiden opened a portal, the entrance to a secret tunnel leading to a cave at Caledonia. The windy passage blew so hard they had to bend into the wind to remain upright. Callan's warning to "watch your step" blew away.

They rested in the cave after Aiden introduced them to Ian, the guard on duty. Ilsa tended to Mairi, wrapping her ankle. All of them drank from their flasks to restore their strength. Mairi had bruises, but Ilsa wrapped her ankle so she could manage a slow walk.

The tall trees and the cave fell behind them as they traversed long grasses in front of them. They could see trees ahead of them in the distance. They walked an hour before reaching an apple grove. They stopped after the apple grove and before the pear grove, both laden with fruit which was expected in the fall, not the spring. It was Kayleigh's first time seeing apple and pear trees.

Aiden handed Kayleigh a pear. "A sweet for the sweet," he said.

"I must have been ten the last time you said those words," Kayleigh said, nostalgia rising within her heart.

"It was your tenth birthday, and I was being nice to you then. You were too distracting after it."

"We're having a break, everyone. Callan, we're ready for the big blanket. We're having a fruit break. Everyone eat an apple or a pear. It will increase your stamina. Caledonia is filled with such beauty and abundance as this," said Aiden.

"We also have an abundance of potted apple and pear sauces, jams, and compotes. They last through the year," Callan said.

"Ah, it's nice to sit," said Kayleigh as she sank onto the blanket. "Mmm. What a lovely place. It's the best pear I ever ate." When finished, she lay back on the blanket next to Mairi.

Her eyes closed, and she felt a presence at her head. She opened them and saw Aiden gathering the refuse. She warmed as their eyes met. *His face is so serene. What a gentle look in his eyes.* She felt her face flush. *Such a sweet smile.* Her shyness abated, and she smiled right back at him. *He's glowing.* Her smile deepened. He stood. *Too bad he's not wearing a kilt. Thank goodness he doesn't read minds. If he had, then my sixteen-year-old self would have been embarrassed all the time he visited.*

"You okay?" Aiden said.

"I'm good. When I was sixteen, how old were you?" Kayleigh said.

"Help her, and let's get going." Callan reached out to help her stand, though Aiden nudged him aside.

"Twenty-one. And enchanted with your sixteen-year-old self," Aiden said and grasped her hand in his sticky one.

"Eew!"

Callan laughed.

Aiden poured water on a cloth to wipe her hands.

Even Mairi giggled.

"Feeling better?" Brighde said.

"I feel stronger. It must be the food. I can feel it

running through my blood," Mairi said.

"It's wonderful," Brighde said. "Isn't it, Kayleigh?"

"Yes, it's good. The warmer air must also be helping."

The group resumed their journey and walked for a couple of hours, passing cottages and people working in the fields. Aiden's clan welcomed them as if used to seeing visitors. A smile, a nod, a friendly wave, and a return to the activity. Most women wore the sleeves on their blouses rolled. The men wore kilts. Most worked in gardens and on crops or with livestock. They passed a carpenter building a table and a potter with his kiln.

"The group of women over there is making a peach-colored dye," Aiden said.

Everyone they passed greeted them.

"Visitors are uncommon in Caledonia. Graeme must have sent word out to expect us," Aiden said.

Nearing the manor, Kayleigh saw a man larger than Aiden. Even Callan was a tall man but appeared short in comparison.

Graeme greeted his brothers with crushing hugs. He was half a head taller than Aiden with the same build but with bright auburn hair. "Welcome home, all," he said in a deep voice.

Lavender and bluebells grew inside the border walls, creating a beautiful garden. They entered the two-story manor-style house with a central hall and two wings. They followed the housekeeper to a large table already set for them with chicken noodle soup, bread, butter, cheese, and pitchers of ale. The blue pitchers and cups matched the blue flowers on the plates.

Kayleigh watched as Graeme leaned on the table and directed his gaze in Mairi's direction. "My sympathy, Madam. Your needs will be met here at Caledonia. If you lack anything, you will come to me. Aye?"

"Aye, Sir."

"Graeme. Use my name, madam, if you do not mind."

"Please. I am Mairi."

"As you wish. Mairi." He gave a slight bow. "The infirmary has been prepared for your arrival. You will sleep in a warm bed tonight. Rooms were prepared for each of you."

Kayleigh noted the warm, gentle voice he used with Mairi. As if she would break were he to use the voice that had greeted Aiden. Perhaps some matchmaking here would be welcomed. Brighde's scheming look revealed she shared her thoughts.

"Welcome to our clan, sisters."

"Thank you," Kayleigh said.

"Many thanks," Brighde echoed.

Kayleigh wondered when it would start to feel like home.

****

Aiden offered Kayleigh his arm. "I need to show you to your room." He led her upstairs. "I have a gift for you."

A gift? They were not in the habit of gift-giving.

He opened the door, and they were greeted with a full-throated meow.

"A cat! You knew I needed one." She scanned the room but didn't see it. A huge bed dominated the room. She responded to the emphatic meow-ow at her feet. Robbie himself leaped into her arms. His chest rumbled, and whiskers rubbed her chin. He repeated the motion even when her tears fell. She sat on the quilt-covered bed, still holding him.

"Aiden." Her voice shook with emotion. "Sit."

He sat with his arm behind her.

"You wonderful man. Such a thoughtful gift. The best."

"I know you missed him and wanted to give you a gift and a smidgen of happiness."

"I'm grateful, Aiden, for everything."

"But the massacre, I was unable to prevent it, even with Will Campbell's warning."

"You saved Aunt Ilsa, Brighde, Mairi, Fiona, and the other women, children, and men. We don't know how many would have died if you hadn't spread the news. You succeeded. From the bottom of my heart, I thank you. I'm grateful for my life." She could lose herself in his warm, blue eyes. And would welcome it.

"Is this my mother's quilt?"

"Considering the wee lad's feelings—he occupied the quilt—we brought it to Caledonia with us," said Aiden.

"Considering his feelings?"

"Aye. Cats demand a gentle touch."

"I suspect you were afraid of being scratched."

He started to shake his head *no* but switched to a nod with a grin. And sighed. "Cat scratches sting more than removing an arrow from torn flesh. Should anyone hear word of this weakness, I will know you betrayed me."

"I'll not betray you. Your secret is safe."

"Just be sure it stays safe." He smiled, showing his perfect, clean teeth.

"How can you think I would ever betray you?"

"You don't know what you are saying." He pet

Robbie, who hissed at him.

"Ha! Robbie knows I speak the truth."

"You always speak the truth."

"As do you."

"I fear I'm not as honest as you are," said Aiden.

"Have you lied to me?"

He took her hand in his. "I have feelings for you."

"Now you're teasing. You know I have my own true love to find."

"Indeed, you do. Will you let me know when you find him?"

"You'll be the first to know besides him."

****

They had a dinner of pot roast, boiled potatoes, beets, and beans. Dessert was apple turnovers.

After dinner on the second day, they discussed the tasks they would help with.

"I volunteer to dust and sweep the floors," Kayleigh said.

"No, it's not the right fit," Aiden said.

"Oh yes, I would like time to practice my archery."

"No. I mean, yes. But there's more."

"What? It isn't enough?"

"I want you to volunteer to be on the guard patrol. Your skills fit in with this duty. It would be the day patrol. I gathered all your archery equipment and brought it here," Aiden replied. "Raibert and Debra reported you're a fierce warrior, tireless in protecting the women and children. They were safe with you. The women considered you their protector and asked Debra to give you their thanks."

"Your keen vision swept the valley. You guided us through the tunnels, a steep climb," Brighde added.

"The women were steadfast in all ways. They deserve credit. The arduous climb to Coire Gabhail, cave conditions, sharing tasks through the long wait. Bravery in the face of uncertainty. They were amazing. I just kept watch," Kayleigh indicated.

"You are one of those women you call brave. You led us in all you say."

Brighde turned to the others. "She can shoot the arrow from the back of a horse, sitting or standing."

Mairi nodded her head in agreement. "I saw it back at home.

"Many women I watched began to crumble until they looked at you. Seeing you, they sat straighter, strengthened by your presence," Brighde added.

Mairi said, "Yes, I saw the same thing. You inspired the women to greatness."

"All this praise overwhelms me," said Kayleigh. "Of course, I will serve as needed. I am humbled by your words. It is a great responsibility."

"What about the men?" Callan asked.

"What do you mean?" Aiden poured more ale into his cup.

"The men may not like me being on patrol with them, and I wear trews, as you know." Kayleigh crossed her arms in front of her chest.

"Caledonia treats men and women as equals," Aiden reminded them.

"You may have trouble," Graeme reached for the pitcher of ale. "You are new leadership since you have accepted, and bringing a woman into the guard may cause trouble."

"The guard is trained to obey orders, and they will. I'll handle any trouble." Aiden hit his hand on the table.

"I will support you in this," Graeme said.

"I'm glad we are all being supportive," Callan said.

"Will you support volunteering Brighde to the stables?" Graeme asked, raising his eyebrows.

"I wouldn't like this, Graeme," Brighde interrupted, her cheeks flushed.

"What do you prefer?" Graeme asked.

"I'd like to work in the home, and Ilsa and Mairi are fine needleworkers, true artists."

"Perhaps Mairi and Ilsa would do mending and their artistry. Would you do the dusting and sweeping of our private quarters?"

"Yes, it would be nice," Brighde said.

Mairi and Ilsa agreed.

"There it is. Good work, all," Graeme said.

Chapter 4

Aiden and Kayleigh had been patrolling together during the days.

"Here we are. My favorite tree," Kayleigh said. "I enjoy our late morning breaks."

"A beautiful tree. Why your favorite?" Aiden asked.

"Its energy is serene. Here, let's sit."

They sat side by side against the tree.

"Do you like patrolling?" Aiden took an apple turnover from his satchel, broke it in half, and offered it to Kayleigh.

"Yes, why do you ask?" Kayleigh replied and smiled. "Dessert first?"

He grinned and nodded. "I'm thinking Bryan might not appreciate patrolling. He might like to change assignments."

"What makes you think so?"

"The man loves horses. I've been thinking about this. He spends his spare time at the stables, feeds the horses, helps exercise them," Aiden brushed the crumbs from his kilt. "Have you ever had the honor of patrolling with him?"

"You know you assign me to you and always have, ever since I've been in Caledonia." Kayleigh shook the crumbs from her hands and wiped them with a cloth he gave her.

He folded the cloth and returned it to his sporran.

"Ah, yes, and it will always be so. The man loves horses. I'm told he talks about them while patrolling. He might be grateful to move to a stable position with Callan."

"Of course. He would also appreciate Callan's light-hearted demeanor and his sense of humor. Then there's—"

"Enough about Callan." He turned her head for a brief kiss, which landed on her cheek. "Have any of the men bothered you?"

"You mean—"

"Have they made remarks about your pants?"

"These?" She indicated her loose-fitting trews. "No."

"Have they touched you in any way?"

"No. Of course not! They are friendly." She pushed him with both hands. *He must be joking.*

"Are you sure? Maybe you don't understand Caledonian ways."

"Aiden, stop. I assure you I have not been made to feel unwelcome in any way. People smile at me."

"What do we have to eat?"

Kayleigh opened the bag.

"Bread and cheese. My favorite meal," he said.

"You can't fool me. I saw the way you devoured the pot roast last night. Is it not your favorite?" She handed him the larger piece of cheese with bread.

"Uh oh. You caught me in a half-truth. As cheese and bread are the customary fare for snacking, it must be my favorite. The choices are limited. Granted, my logic is flawed." His clear blue eyes lit with humor.

"Logic doesn't apply to food favorites. I didn't like when our tutor insisted we study logic."

"It wasn't fair of him to require us to use it in

everyday life." Aiden sighed.

"I remember when Aunt Ilsa had enough of logic. She forbade me to use it." She giggled.

"Remind me. How long did you live with Ilsa?"

"She moved in with us when her husband passed before I was born. Then, after my mother passed, she managed our home. Father wasn't around much, so her being with us was fortunate. I last saw him on the morning of my sixth birthday."

"I remember the sad day."

"What I remember most was the feeling of being hopeful and then hope being killed all day while I waited for him. You see, he promised to be there. It broke my heart when bedtime came, and he hadn't come home. He never did come home. Aunt Ilsa held me as I cried. It was the first time I cried so hard."

"I remember. We were there, Callan and me. It was a sad day watching you and Brighde waiting for him." He put his arm around her and squeezed her shoulder. "I'm sorry I raised the memory. Let's change the subject, okay?"

She held back her tears. "Yes."

"Hmm…let's see. What do you value about me?"

"You are honest and honorable."

"A good answer. But not because you are attracted to my looks?"

"Your value is not in your looks, but in who you are. You are more than your handsome self. And shame on you for fishing for a compliment."

"You think I am handsome?"

"You think I'm lying?"

"I trust you to tell the truth as you see it. Your eyes…"

He tucked her hair behind her ear and stroked her cheek and chin. His finger touched her lips.

"My eyes tell the truth?"

"You tell the truth. Your eyes are beautiful, the color of Graeme's finest imported whiskey."

"Whiskey, hmm?"

"Your hair is the color of the rare cinnamon Rose buys at market."

She laughed. "No. You exaggerate. There is no red in my hair. It is brown, like a mouse, but shinier."

"Cinnamon isn't red. It's more amber and is essential to many fine recipes, and your hair being cinnamon is beautiful."

"You are attracted to my looks, which is appreciated. There should be more, though."

"You know for certain I value your skills. There may be many pretty faces in the world, but yours is the one to which I'm drawn. And I know for a fact you are kind." He stood before she could. "Let's get back to patrolling." He put the bag in his sporran. Then he took her hand to help her and handed her the bow and quiver. Her smile was a bright burst of sunlight, like the summer sunrise at Coire Gabhail.

****

They sat together beneath their favorite tree for a snack, even when not patrolling.

"I enjoy our time together," Aiden stroked her hand.

"I do, too." Kayleigh squeezed his fingers and pulled away.

"My affection for you is growing."

"We grow closer all of the time," Kayleigh said.

"It's more than this. It's what you might call romantic affection."

"It can't be. I'm handfasted to someone else."

"I have always been attracted to you and have always cared for you."

"I can't return a romantic affection. Even if I am attracted to you, my affection is as a friend. I have always cared for you too."

"We can discuss this further another day."

"Or maybe not."

****

Kayleigh finished her snack alone for the first time. *Where is he? I suppose it would be kind to bring him his snack.* She stood and wiped her crumbs to the ground. She walked along, noticing the wildflowers, trying not to step on them. *If I'm not careful, a path will be worn through the grass.* She stepped in a zig-zag fashion. If she zig-zagged or took a circular route every time, it could prevent the path. It seemed Glencoe had more paths than Caledonia. The pang in her heart longed for home. But home was no more.

Who are they? A man and woman shouldn't be wrapped around each other in public for all to see. She walked closer and stopped short. *It's Aiden.* Her heart sped. *With Fiona wrapped around him. His hands on her waist, his head bent. He's better than this. He's supposed to be an honest and honorable man. Kissing on patrol, on our break time. And here I am, kind enough to bring him his snack. What a rat! This is how he repays me?*

Infused with anger, she approached him and threw the satchel at his feet. "Your food."

She started to turn away but saw he was struggling to get Fiona loose. She marched up to them, grabbed the woman by her hair, and pulled her off Aiden. "You will hereafter not accost Aiden. Understood?" The woman started to shake her head *no* but looked Kayleigh in the eyes, turned her gaze to the bow she carried, looked at her face again, and nodded her head, scurrying away backward, then turned in a full-out run.

"I thought to bring lunch to an overworked chief, and I find him wrapped around a woman. Chief, you might consider watching where you wander."

"I was going to meet you for lunch when she accosted me. Jealousy doesn't become you."

"I'm not jealous. I have better sense than to believe you, the patrol chief, would engage in flirtation while on the job. You should be aware of Fiona and her feminine wiles."

"Point taken. But I didn't fall for her wiles or anything else. Don't accuse me."

"I didn't intend to accuse you. Eat your food. And good day!" And she turned around and left to return to her post.

"Thank you for the meal!" He hurried after her.

She gestured with the derogatory hand signal the men used with each other and continued walking.

****

Sitting back against the tree, Kayleigh unwrapped the food, revealing the single portion she'd brought. Aiden frowned his disappointment. Kayleigh took a bite of cheese, filling her cheek, having difficulty chewing, and stuffed in a piece of bread.

Eyebrows raised in disbelief, he watched her eat. "I apolo…"

"What were you going to say?"

"Again, I apologize for yesterday. May I have a share of the food?"

She gave him half of what was left. "I wasn't sure I

would have company today. But here, you can have half of mine." They ate, their usual banter silenced. She reached into the sack and took out the one sweet she had brought. "Though the patrol chief must eat, he needs no sweet."

His eyes shining, he checked the wrapping to be sure there wasn't one for him.

"Don't cry. There's nothing worse than a man crying over a sweet." She tore it and gave him half of the apple turnover. She stood upon finishing, grabbed her bow and quiver, and set off to patrol. She left the wrappings for him to discard, stopped, and turned to wait for him. "It's your turn to bring a snack tomorrow, two portions. No cheese and bread."

"Right. Will do. Let's resume patrol."

****

The next day, there were hot meat pies. To keep the meal warm, Aiden took Kayleigh to the stables. She met Bryan and his young son Gabriel. Kayleigh heard his tummy grumbling.

"Here, you can have my meat pie," said Kayleigh. She split her pie, giving half to Gabriel and a quarter each to Bryan and Callan.

Gabriel gobbled his pie, and the men ate theirs in two bites.

Aiden gave Kayleigh half of his pie. "You may have it on the condition you eat it."

She gave her dessert to the boy, sticking her hand out to Aiden, who surrendered his for the two men.

He pulled out two flasks of ale and gave one for Callan to share. "Here's a flask for you. I'll share mine with Kayleigh."

I felt hungry all the time when Father was

37

unproductive. But since Bryan is productive, why is this boy so hungry? There's plenty of food for everyone at Caledonia.

She took the flask from Aiden and tipped ale into the boy's mouth. "Didn't anyone give you food this morning?"

Callan said, "We ate our oatcakes early because Gabe was so hungry."

"Oatcakes? From now on, you will receive enough food for the work you do. Both of you will come to the manor for the evening meal, right, Aiden?"

"Yes, you are most welcome at the table."

"Gabriel will be dropped off at the manor before the work hour to break his fast and to study with Brighde, join in meals, and play with the other children, right Aiden?"

"Yes, it seems a fair and creative solution."

"Bryan and Callan will bring enough food to the stables so their stomachs don't grumble until the evening meal. Bryan will take meals with Callan. Bryan has no one to cook food at home. I am sure Graeme will agree. After all, he helps women who are alone and the elderly. He will now help men who are alone. And their children, right, Aiden?"

"Yes, I am certain Graeme will agree."

"Helping the men must become a rule like it is for the women. Otherwise, the men will be too proud to come, right Callan?"

He looked at her, surprise written on his face. "Yes, yes indeed. They might be too proud."

She heard Aiden brag about her as she walked away. "The lass does like to make decisions. She understands it as one of her guard duties."

She gave a satisfied snort. *He will learn to keep the bragging to himself. I'll not correct him in front of the men. Not for something so pleasant.*

Chapter 5

After dinner one evening, Kayleigh started to go downstairs and stopped at what she heard.

"Do you think she should be sent away?" Graeme said.

"It might be a bit too harsh," Aiden said.

Callan spoke next. "A bit too harsh? How can something be a bit harsh? Either it is, or it isn't."

"Okay. It's too harsh," Aiden agreed.

"The woman plays fast and loose with the men," Graeme said.

She heard Aiden's sigh. "She's just looking for love and doesn't know how to go about it."

Is this what he thinks of me? I am interested in the other men? I only love him. Love? No, not love. Does he think I am playing with him? How can he think I am loose... I'll show him loose. Maybe Bryan...eew... It's not like anything's wrong with him...yes there is...he's not Aiden... I'll show him.

She rushed downstairs and stopped in shock.

"We've only ever been friends. She has our relationship wrong. She might follow me around everywhere, but I have never been interested in her." Aiden shifted to make room next to him.

"You lie! You have misled me, you liar! Graeme, he lies to you!" said Kayleigh, as she remained standing, waving her arms.

Callan burst out laughing.

"You misheard us talking about—" Graeme shook his head no.

"We weren't talking about you," Aiden said. "Fiona—"

"Fiona! She's the last person you should be with. You want fast and loose?" Kayleigh looked around the room. "Where is Bryan?"

"Bryan? Do you think she would be interested?" Graeme wiped his hands as if finished with the talk.

"Great idea, Kayleigh!" Aiden smiled congratulations at her, seemingly pleased with her.

"Kayleigh," Callan said. "It's not you. It's—"

"Yes. Bryan's the answer to the problem," Aiden said.

Kayleigh's tears would not be held back. *I can't believe they think so little of me. And Callan is laughing at me.*

"Fiona. You would saddle him with Fiona? He's a good man," said Aiden. "Kayleigh, why are you crying?"

"She's crying?" Graeme looked confused. "Why?"

"Kayleigh, you don't understand," Callan interrupted.

She had their attention and hiccupped. The tears just wouldn't stop. She wiped her eyes with her shirt sleeve.

"Kayleigh thought you were talking about her. Sending her away… fast and loose…" Callan said, now serious.

"Kayleigh!" Aiden said. "I would never speak ill of you. None of it would apply to you. You are the opposite of Fiona."

"The opposite," Graeme said, nodding his agreement.

"Everything we said was about Fiona," Callan said. "Truly."

"It was?" Kayleigh sniffled.

"Yes," Callan said.

"Indeed," Aiden nodded.

"Yes," Graeme smiled.

"Why is a woman the problem here? She is looking for her forever love. It's the men who are 'playing fast and loose' with Fiona," Kayleigh said. She was surprised all of them were listening to her. "Always, you men and many women blame women for these things. When it's the men who are making the woman think they are serious. Why aren't the men blamed?"

"You make a good point," Aiden indicated, lifting his drink. "We need to curb our language when speaking of Fiona."

"You mean women, not just Fiona. Be aware of how you speak about women," Kayleigh said. "Right?"

"Yes."

"Agreed."

"And it's not enough. When others blame women or use inappropriate language about women, you should correct them."

"I don't know," Graeme said. "It would cause trouble with the men. They need our support."

"Don't they take criticism in their jobs? It's their top responsibility." Aiden added, "Their families are top priority, but they seem to hold their jobs in higher esteem. If they can bear being criticized in their job, they should be able to bear being corrected."

"You make a good point. We will make corrections as needed. And we will make no exceptions, even with each other." Graeme's hand slapped the table, making everyone jump.

"Now. About Bryan… It may be a good match. He is a good man, and he is what Fiona needs." Aiden stood next to Kayleigh.

"We're not going to do matchmaking," Graeme said.

"Surely there is no harm in two people getting to know one another," Aiden said.

"Unless their names are Aiden and Kayleigh," Callan teased.

Brighde entered the room in time to hear the matchmaking discussion. She marched over to Callan and hit him on the arm. "She's my sister. Keep your mean thoughts to yourself."

"Then I wouldn't be me, would I?" he said.

"Back to the topic," Brighde said. "Fiona and Bryan might make a good match. What would be the harm in seating them at the same table?"

"She would displace someone else," Graeme argued.

Michael and Lorna were seen walking together after dinner. Move him from Bryan's table to her table. It would solve the problem," Brighde said.

"Good idea, Sister!" Kayleigh laughed, pleased with the problem's resolution.

****

After dinner one day, Rose entered the Hall with a man who looked distressed.

"Graeme, this is Gerald, the beekeeper," Rose said. "He needs another ration of salt."

Graeme spoke, "Tell me what happened to your ration."

"Last time, the man brought twice as much salt. I

43

gave him an extra ration of honey, as you ordered."

"I didn't order it. Who is this man?"

"I'm not a rat."

"You know you have to tell me. You've been diverting honey to the man. He's using expensive salt."

"It's Angus. He must have a bigger ration of salt than me. He gave me an extra ration of salt."

"Rose, have we been missing salt?" Graeme asked.

"It seems we have been running low," Rose said. "I thought we were using more because we've more mouths to feed."

"It's not your fault, Rose."

Callan entered the room holding the arm of a man who held the bottle of salt. "I thought this would be a perfect time for the thief to strike."

"Angus, give the salt to Rose."

Rose returned to the kitchen with the salt.

"Gerald, why do you need the extra salt?" Graeme questioned the supposed thief.

"As you know, it's valuable. My Sarah is pregnant and craves sweets. Her ankles are big now, so she can't stand long enough to bake sweets. The salt is used to buy pies and biscuits and extra food from our neighbors. They want to help but can't afford to feed two more mouths plus one on the way," Gerald said.

Angus reported, "My wife is expecting and also craves sweets. So, we need the extra honey. It's why I stole the salt. I know it's wrong, but I want to keep my wife happy."

"Salt is not a currency. We at Caledonia spend good money to have the luxury of salt, enough for everyone to season our food, along with the other herbs and spices. On another note, when a woman is expecting, food rations increase. This includes honey. This has always been our practice. Mention it to Rose so she can correct the situation. Tell others about this practice."

Callan commented, "I see an increase of babies in our future."

Ilsa frowned at Callan. "Gerald, Sarah has a medical condition which can be dangerous. Salt makes the condition worse. Neighbors should be told not to salt the food they prepare for you. You can always add salt to your own food, but not to Sarah's. You should see her ankles return closer to normal, and she will be much happier. I would tell you to limit her sweets, but an expecting mother needs to satisfy her cravings."

"Come with me, Gerald," said Graeme. "You need to pay your neighbors for preparing food. This will not be a regular practice. It's an exception because of Sarah's medical condition," said Graeme. "Since she also needs to stay in bed, your home will be cleaned by the manor staff twice a week until the babe is born, and she can take on such tasks. If more is needed, let me know. While you work, have a neighbor visit with her for a time. You and I will decide how much to pay for each task. I'll give you two weeks at a time. Come." And the door shut.

"You left the salt for anyone to help himself." Rose's voice could be heard from the kitchen. "What's wrong with you? Do you want to keep this job, or do you want to be a gardener?"

"I want to be a kitchen worker."

Aiden intervened and entered the kitchen. His voice could be heard through the door. It was always loud. "Rose, please don't scold Anna. We're equals here, and everyone deserves a tone of respect. And if you heard me speaking that way, you should correct me. The salt situation doesn't reflect on you or Anna. It was the work of a clever man in a tight situation, not being able to provide for his family. Not everyone knows all of our rules. They live far from the manor and enter new situations without guidance. Be well and trust one another." He entered the Hall.

As the door opened and closed, Kayleigh heard Rose. "I'm sorry, lass, you know I am. I'm glad you agreed to work with me. I'm glad you're here."

"Apology accepted. We do well together," Anna said.

"Will we also increase the ration of whiskey?" Callan wondered aloud.

"No," Aiden responded. "We would have to give an extra bottle per family. It's too much. They each have a share now."

"Graeme handled the situation well," Kayleigh said.

"He tries to see all sides of a situation and wants justice served," Aiden noted.

"I'm impressed with how things are run in Caledonia," Brighde said.

"Being located away from others, we must make sure everyone is treated fairly. Graeme is willing to hear complaints and suggestions. This helps him as a leader," Aiden agreed.

"Our Graeme's not just a good brother. He's a good leader too," Callan nodded in further agreement.

****

Sitting with Aiden under the serene tree, Kayleigh noticed his silence.

"I can't stand it. What's wrong?" She shifted to see his face.

"Nothing." Aiden denied any problems.

46

"You don't talk to me," she said.

"I don't have anything to say."

"To me? In all my life, when have you ever had nothing to say?"

"Here," he said. He stood and took her hand. "Stand here with me for a minute."

He held both hands and looked into her eyes.

He bent his head until his clear blue eyes were a cup's distance from hers. He looked at her lips and parted his. He closed the distance between them and brushed her lips. Then he kissed her with passion. Sparks traveled her spine.

"Every time we're alone, this is what I'm thinking. Kisses. And more."

She blinked in wonder and reached out to kiss him with her new passion. He pulled her close and slanted his mouth on her lips in one direction, then the other. His kisses grew more ardent.

"You see, I am preoccupied with this, with how it could be between us," he said.

"If you're thinking about this all the time, I can see why you seem distant. Please stop thinking about it." She moved away from him.

"Men think about this sort of thing most of the time. It is not unusual."

"Maybe we need to change patrolling partners."

"No. I won't trust another man to keep his hands off you."

"Not even Ian, who has a fondness for Rose? Or Callan?"

"I would trust Callan, but he's not on patrol. Ian can appreciate a beautiful woman. His attention would be diverted to you for the duration of the patrol, which could be detrimental to getting the job done. I may be distant, but I can do the job in your presence."

"I see. You are not immune to me but can control yourself."

"Yes."

"The distance I see is the result of the distance you must keep from me for fear I might seduce you."

"Yes. No. I am not afraid of you in any way. You are Kayleigh, who I have known your entire life."

"Then you no longer need to remain distant. It is just me, who I have always been."

"I wanted you when you were younger."

"I should do knitting instead of patrolling. Or I could plant lavender with Brighde. Maybe Mairi would teach me needlepoint. It must be easier than knitting. There are many things. Whisky making is another."

"You're not going anywhere near the whisky making. You will be patrolling with me. Unless it is a hardship."

She laughed. "Now, there's a fine bit of teasing. How does it feel?"

"You made your point."

"I want to continue patrolling with you. Since I know your mind better, I'll know when your thoughts are distracted and can redirect them."

They sat again, and Kayleigh gave bits of cheese and bread to the squirrels in front of her.

"Kayleigh, you're going to need to stop feeding the squirrels," said Aiden. "They're starting to go to people looking for choice tidbits."

"I love the squirrels. They're so cute, and they're intelligent."

"They're not intelligent. Only human beings are

intelligent."

She stood up to argue with him, hands on her hips. "They recognize me and know I have their best interests at heart."

"You are simply a food source."

"They have families. They have husbands and wives."

"Do they have rituals? Religion? Language?"

"We do not know. Just because we don't understand their language, it doesn't mean they don't have one," said Kayleigh. "Listen to them. Is it not their language?"

"Okay, I give in. They have their own language."

"They must also read minds, each others' minds."

"I'll grant you they have body language, but we can't know if they read one anothers' minds."

"They enjoy the food. And even you must see they enjoy it as a treat."

"They're becoming pests."

"They're sweet and interesting."

"Maybe sweet though I doubt it. Interesting, yes," said Aiden.

"I will continue to save them tidbits of bread and cheese from my breakfast."

"Just don't ask me to do the same."

She laughed. "I wouldn't dream of it, though it's a funny thought. You, feeding squirrels."

Chapter 6

Leaning against the serene tree, they finished lunch. Aiden was about to kiss Kayleigh when he heard the familiar sound of a bowstring twanging and arrow launching. Aiden fell to protect her, coming between her and the arrow sticking out of his shoulder.

"Move, stay low, run to the manor!" Aiden shot out orders she obeyed without hesitation. He was grateful for her training and heard men running away from the scene in different directions, but his priority was to get her to safety. One attacker was bad enough. Two was unthinkable.

Brighde and Callan were outside sitting by the gardens when they arrived at the manor.

"Aiden! What happened?" Callan said, with Brighde by his side.

Kayleigh grabbed Aiden's other hand and tried to drag him inside. "An arrow happened. Can't you see it? Two men ran away. Send the guards by the serene tree!" She hurried him to the infirmary, grasping his hand.

"It's flaming hot. Is there poison on it?" asked Aiden.

"An arrow wound burns even without poison. You would be on the ground if you were poisoned," said Kayleigh.

He looked at her in surprise.

"We had a poisoning at Glencoe when I was a child.

It was a horrible death, though what death isn't horrible?"

Ilsa entered the room with hot water, towels, and an ointment. "Calendula and honey," she stated.

Graeme came in to cut and remove the arrow. Callan came in with the whiskey. "A cup to drink, a cup for the wound." He handed them to Aiden and Ilsa. "Not to worry, Kayleigh. Aiden's a quick healer. He'll feel better tomorrow night and will be able to use his shoulder the next day."

She grunted in disbelief.

Aiden drank the whiskey, draining the cup in two swallows.

"Serene tree?" Callan asked.

Graeme corrected him. "Kissing tree."

"Kissing tree! I'm going to hit your other shoulder! All this time, we have been snacking under the kissing tree? How could you?" said Kayleigh.

Graeme chuckled. Callan out and out laughed.

"You'd better not be repeating your old shenanigans, brother," Graeme said to Aiden.

"No." Aiden managed to get it out with a loud groan as the arrow was removed.

Kayleigh held his hand, patting it. She noticed the ring lying in his chest hair.

"You have a ring around your neck like I do," said Kayleigh.

He mumbled, "Mine own true love."

"Yes, Aiden has his own true love, just like you do," said Callan.

"Does he know who she is?" said Kayleigh.

"Yes," said Callan.

"Why aren't they married then?"

"She's not ready yet."

"Mine own true…" said Aiden.

Aiden passed out as Ilsa poured whiskey into his wound.

"He just went under," said Callan. "And secrets will remain secrets."

"Callan, hold your tongue," said Graeme.

Brighde and Kayleigh exchanged questioning looks and shrugged.

Kayleigh's tears threatened to fall. She tried not to blink without success.

Brighde put her arms around Kayleigh. "He will be okay. Ilsa will take care of him."

Aiden had his own true love? He must be flirting with me when he says romantic things. But he protected me from the arrow. He got me to the keep, leaving the archers for the guards. It fits in with our training, getting the victim to safety. I wasn't the victim, though. He was. But he fell across me and took the arrow for me. So, maybe I was the victim. He's an honorable man and honest. So why flirt with me?

"It's going to be okay. They will find the man who did this," said Graeme.

Kayleigh stood there in the infirmary as it all sank into her. Shock, disbelief.

Oh my God, look at him. Strong, hairy chest, muscled arms, and shoulders. She winced. *Flat muscled abdomen with a feathery line of hair leading to… Oh goodness. I want him.*

Callan took her arm to lead her out. "Stop your drooling, dear, before he awakens, and you see just how quick you get a rise out of him."

She felt the flush suffuse her cheeks.

"Enough, Callan," Graeme said. "You go too far."

Even Brighde frowned at him. "Come with me, dear," she said to Kayleigh. "Let Ilsa care for him. You need a cup and then rest. You'll feel much better after retiring. Then we'll visit with Aiden.

Kayleigh allowed herself to be led away.

****

On the next day, Aiden insisted on eating dinner with everyone.

"What will happen to the man who shot Aiden?" Kayleigh asked after the meal.

"It will depend on what Aiden wants, though I suspect he will want rehabilitation instead of punishment," Graeme indicated.

"It's always preferable to heal someone rather than exact a harsh punishment," Aiden said. "Harsh punishment can produce adverse results in the person."

"We haven't ever used the dungeon," Graeme reminded.

"It's refreshing to hear," Mairi quietly shared.

"It's good news," Brighde agreed.

"Hmph," Kayleigh grunted.

"You disagree? Graeme makes the ultimate decision," Aiden said. "Though he consults with us and the person wronged."

Kayleigh expressed her doubt. "If a dungeon is not an option, how can you be taken seriously?"

"It's not like no punishment is given. We try to avoid harsh punishment unless it is warranted. Please pass the pitcher of ale." He received it as it was passed along the table. "Thanks, Callan."

"Then why have a dungeon?"

"We think it would be useful should raiders reach

Caledonia. A Caledonian might get time in jail and, at the worst, be exiled."

Rose and Anna brought out trays of pear compote and apple turnovers to set on the tables, with a pile of biscuits for the children.

"Suppose a Glencoe MacDonald shot Aiden? What would happen to him?" Kayleigh wondered.

"It would be a new situation worthy of much discussion," Aiden responded.

"Wouldn't a punishment depend on the intention of the attacker?"

"It would be taken into consideration," said Callan.

At the end of the table, Bryan seemed to be scolding Gabriel, who shouted, "It was an accident!"

Silence followed.

"What would happen if it was an accident?" Bryan asked.

Aiden said, "It would depend on why the arrow was shot. If negligence, then a form of punishment might be needed."

"Gabriel, why did you shoot Mr. Aiden?" Kayleigh queried.

"I didn't shoot him! I missed."

"Aiden has an injury. I was there and saw the arrow. I watched Mr. Graeme take it out of his shoulder," said Kayleigh.

"I didn't mean to shoot him."

"Why did you shoot your arrow?"

"I saw the snake. He was going to shoot you." The child was shaking.

"The snake was going to bite me?"

"No. Yes. The mansnake was going to shoot you. So I shot him, and I missed."

"Since the arrow hit me, I will continue the questioning. Good job, Kayleigh," Aiden interrupted.

Kayleigh nodded at him. *I am a guard, after all. Of course I question criminals. But Gabe is not a criminal. Poor boy thought he was shooting a snake. He tried to protect me.* Her heart warmed at the thought.

"It is always a good idea to protect a lady," Aiden said

"She is your lady. I had to do it." Gabriel stood on a seat, fists clenched, and his father holding him steady.

Oh dear.

"It remains to be seen," Aiden said, his eyes meeting Kayleigh's. "For now, she is her own lady."

"And Miss Brighde's lady," Gabriel added.

"Yes, she is Brighde's sister."

"I don't have a sister or a brother. Or a mother. I have a father. His name is Bryan."

Bryan whispered in Gabe's ear.

"I don't want to talk about the snake. He was big and hairy. He scared me." Gabe held onto Bryan as he sat.

"He was hairy?" Aiden asked.

"You have to catch him! The mansnake wants to hurt Miss Kay—"

Silent until then, Brighde interrupted. "Gabe dear, you keep saying mansnake. Tell me, is the snake a man?"

"Yes. That's what I said."

"So we're looking for a man," Aiden said. "Can you describe him?"

"He was big and hairy." Gabe sounded frustrated.

"Is he big like me or Graeme?" Aiden asked.

"He's big like Mr. Callan."

"And you tried to shoot him? Were you thinking you could hit him?"

"No. I just shot him." Gabe's hands moved to his hips.

"Very good. But you need to work on your aim. Thank you for protecting Kayleigh."

"I had to. She's your lady, and I like her." He mirrored Aiden's stance, arms folded across his chest.

Aiden's eyes caught Kayleigh's. "What color was his hair? Is it long, tied back?"

"He's a MacDonald."

"This narrows the field," Callan said with sarcasm. Brighde shushed him, hitting his arm.

"He wears the MacDonald tartan and a white shirt," Gabriel described the attacker. "Except the shirt isn't white after crawling in the grass."

"Did you see him today after I was shot?" Aiden asked.

"He has red hair and a red nose. And grass on his shirt."

"So, you did see him again."

Gabriel nodded. "Yes."

"Where?"

"On the path with Father."

"When?"

"On the way to dinner."

"Is he in this room?"

"No."

"Are you certain?"

"Yes."

"Let's look again now."

Bryan lifted his son to look around the room.

"No. He's not here."

"If he changed his clothes and combed his hair, would you recognize him?"

"Yes. It's his nose, his drinking nose." Gabe wrinkled his own nose in distaste.

"Oh dear," Brighde sighed. "Gabe knows a drinker's nose."

"The nose has lines in it. Do you think he saw me?"

"Maybe he saw you, but it is more likely he thought you were one of the guards shooting at him," Aiden said. He gave a long look at Kayleigh, then Bryan. "See he gets archer training."

"Gabe's too young for this," Brighde interrupted.

"Apparently not," Aiden said. "He needs to improve his aim."

They left to make a report to the night patrol leader.

****

Kayleigh and Aiden patrolled one night, filling in for Bryan's team. They walked from the manor house to the caves, checked inside the first cave, one hour away, and found remnants of a meal. The second cave was two hours from the first and was always guarded because it led to Coire Gabhail and was the primary entrance to Caledonia. Two or three men always guarded it.

They went into the cave, where Ian guarded the portal.

"Ian, you've met Kayleigh. She'll be patrolling with me tonight. We're covering for Bryan. But we'll still patrol days," Aiden said. "All quiet tonight?"

"Nice to see you, Miss. Nothing to report, sir," Ian said.

"Greetings Ian. Please, call me Kayleigh."

"Did Bryan get his transfer?" he asked.

"Yes, he'll be at the stables from now on," Aiden responded, leaning near the portal.

"He must like the new assignment," Ian said,

mirroring Aiden's movement.

"Of course. He sure loves the horses," Kayleigh said.

"Rose sent an extra snack for you." Aiden handed him a sack. "We'll see you on the way back."

They left the cave and headed to the third cave. It was even farther away, and walking there took two more hours. They heard activity in the third cave as they approached. Kayleigh notched her arrow, set to shoot.

Aiden called out to the intruders. "Come out of the cave. This is the Patrol."

He took a defensive stance where they would stand between him and Kayleigh upon exiting. "Leave any weapons inside. We have you covered."

Two men came out, arms raised, palms facing forward.

"Who are you?" Aiden demanded. "How did you come to be here?"

They turned so they faced the cave, leaving Kayleigh to their right. She moved to the cave entrance, facing them.

"We're Dougal and Roland from Glencoe."

"Dougal, how is it you're here in Caledonia?"

"Grief from losing my Maggie."

"I remember you," Aiden said.

"I also remember Dougal," Kayleigh agreed.

"Since you brought Roland with you, Dougal, you will be responsible for him. No false steps from either of you."

"Yes, sir," Dougal said.

"On your honor," Aiden stated.

"On my honor." Dougal raised his right hand as he spoke.

"On my honor." Roland also raised his hand.

"You have my word. We will be good citizens," Dougal promised.

"First, you need to pass Graeme's scrutiny," Aiden warned.

"Who is Graeme?"

"Who is Graeme?" Kayleigh said. "He's Chief of Caledonia. How long have you been here?"

"A few days. We haven't gone to the village yet."

"You'll go tomorrow," Aiden said. "Trade happens in the village."

"I didn't know." Kayleigh's eyebrows raised, her face animated.

"Since you haven't been to the village, of course, you wouldn't know."

"Missy here admits to not knowing her precious Aiden," Dougal scoffed at her.

"Stop, Dougal. Caledonia was founded many generations ago. Even so, it was founded on the values of respect and equality. Apologize to Kayleigh now," he demanded.

"I apologize," Dougal said, not sounding at all contrite.

"Gather your belongings tomorrow morning and head five hours South," Aiden said. "Ask for Graeme and tell him you are reporting for duty. We have an opening on night patrol. You will patrol with a partner, though not with each other. Get on the rolls with Graeme, and you will be assigned quarters, probably sharing a cabin."

"Will do. Thank you, sir." Dougal bowed.

"Thank you, miss." Roland also bowed.

Aiden and Kayleigh nodded in return. They left after

the two men went into the cave.

They returned to the second cave to see Ian.

"Ron," Aiden said as they reached the entrance to the second cave.

"Ian," Kayleigh said as they neared the portal.

Ian stood, wiping pastry dust from his face.

"Good pastry?" she asked.

"The best, my favorite, apple fritter. Rose's apple fritter is amazing," he said.

"Pears are my favorite," she responded.

They both looked at Aiden, expecting him to answer.

"Apples and pears," he said.

"Apples," she said. "You should see the look on his face when she makes apple turnovers."

"Tell me about Dougal and Roland from Glencoe," Aiden said.

"They came after Kayleigh did."

"What were the circumstances?"

"He, Dougal, lost his wife in the massacre. He was broken about it. Near tears. The other fellow, Roland, had to do most of the talking. Dougal kept crying for Maggie. But then he was able to confirm what the lad said. Said there was nothing left for them in Glencoe. Said Roland was his worker and could contribute to the workings of Caledonia. Said you had told him to come here," Ian said. "It was reported the day they arrived. Two guards brought them in."

"They came after Kayleigh arrived?" Aiden asked. "How long after Kayleigh?"

"Two days," Ian confirmed. "I was on duty both days."

"I did mention Caledonia to him," Aiden said. "But

it puts them here three weeks ago. Why lie about it? What have they been doing all this time they haven't yet gone to the village? They need to check in with Graeme. I'll give them tomorrow and the night. The following day, I'll check with Graeme. If they're not checked in yet, we'll come back to get them."

"I wish we had looked in the last cave," Kayleigh said. "I may remember Dougal, but I don't like him. Never have."

"The way he treats you, I'm not surprised you don't like him," Aiden said. "I don't like him either. He'll find himself exiled if he continues to treat women this way."

"You can exile him just like this?" she asked.

"No. It would take a group of his peers," Ian stated.

"How do you get approved?" Kayleigh wondered.

"They are invited to visit Caledonia," Ian said. "Then the three brothers must agree to approve for the person to stay and become a member."

"Will you vote to approve Dougal?" Kayleigh asked.

"It depends on his behavior," Aiden said.

"How do I become a member of Caledonia?" she asked.

"You are already a member. We approved the group before bringing you," he responded.

"Thank you."

"You're welcome."

"Indeed, you are welcome," Ian said, pushing his hair back.

"Missing this?" Kayleigh retrieved a hair tie from the floor.

"Stay awake, Ian," Aiden said.

"I'm not in the habit of sleeping on the job," he said.

"I know from experience how Rose's pastries act on an empty stomach. They put me into a contented sleep," Aiden said with an exaggerated sigh. "I smell the one you had, and wisps of sleep affect my brain."

"Stay sharp then," Ian teased.

"Our trip back should be uneventful," Aiden said. "I'll be fully alert on leaving your cozy cave."

"Me too. Be safe," Kayleigh said.

They left the cave, and the cold night brought them alert with a jolt.

Kayleigh breathed in the brisk air. The cold bit her nose, and her eyes burned until she secured the scarf she wore. "Thank goodness the daytime weather is more temperate."

"The crisp night air goes through my nose to my brain and through my mouth to my chest. But I can handle it. It's great to have a regular day shift," Aiden agreed.

"You just need a scarf. I'll knit you a scarf."

"You can knit?"

"Ilsa is going to teach me how to knit. How hard could it be? My first project will be a scarf for you. Meanwhile, you can borrow one of my scarves. It's wide and long. A scarf always accents your eyes. So says Brighde."

"Do I need to have my eyes accented?"

"Not at all. They are perfect the way they are. They change, you know."

"What do you mean?"

"Of course, they're blue. They change from the color of the Caledonia sky to the stormy seas of Loch Leven. It happens even indoors. Heated, stormy seas are emotional, and blue skies are calm."

"What color are my eyes regularly? Not calm and not heated eyes?"

"A blue in my quilt, lit from inside."

"All this talk has me wanting to be inside by the fire."

"You want to be cozy. We could sit together by the fire."

"It might be too cozy for me."

"Good ghost, I said cozy, not cuddle," said Kayleigh. "Forget what I said. I'll go upstairs and cuddle with Robbie by my fire with a hot cup of whisky. Yes. Let's hurry back."

"I didn't mean to offend you."

"No one ever means to offend. It's not intention, it's an outcome."

"My offense was a mistake, not intentional, even though it resulted in offending you."

"Oh, for Pete's sake."

"Will you please stop swearing?"

"No. It's not swearing."

"Yes, it is swearing. It's offensive. You swear on Saint Peter."

"No. I swear on Pete."

"It's a shortened version of the original with Saint Peter."

"Why is it offensive? I hear you and Callan swear."

"We're men."

"So, men can swear, and women can't?"

"Right."

"Callan thinks my swearing is endearing."

"Has he said as much?"

"Of course not. It's the way he smiles when I curse."

"He smiles an endearing smile?"

"Yes, exactly."

"Callan is chief of swearing?"

"No. And where is the equality in this?"

"In smiling?"

"No. There is no equality in men being permitted to swear, but women being prohibited from swearing."

"It's not a matter of state. It's personal."

"So, in general, you don't practice equality. It's a matter of state."

"Will you please stop? I apologize for my offense. I already did it once, now twice."

"You are forgiven."

"You give a hard-won forgiveness. I don't think it's supposed to be so difficult."

"It kept us warm out here in the cold night."

"True, it did."

"I would guess your eyes are stormy blue right now."

"You're probably right."

"I'll stop swearing when on patrol, for your sake."

"Thank you."

****

They arrived at the manor house in the wee hours when everyone should have been asleep. Rose brought them cups of warm whisky and plates of food she had warmed in the oven. She'd had a helper on horseback watch for their return and gave her half an hour to prepare for them.

It was much warmer inside the house. Kayleigh unwound her scarf, the MacDonald tartan, balled it, and threw it to Aiden.

He sniffed at it and smiled.

"What? Does it smell like sweat?" Kayleigh asked,

offended.

"It smells like you, very sweet," he said.

"Sweet!"

"Don't get in a fuss about it. I said it smells sweet. I didn't say it was a character flaw."

"My character has no flaws."

"Every character has flaws."

"My main flaw is liking you."

"Don't worry, Kayleigh," Callan said. "He will sleep with the scarf under his pillow, the better to dream of you." He held his hands to his face with his cheek lying on them like a pillow with a dreamy look on his face.

Everyone laughed. Brighde hit his arm and laughed louder.

The joke, though, didn't sit well with Kayleigh.

"Give it back!" she said. "I said give it back."

"No. I want it. I need it until you knit me a scarf." Aiden winked at her. "And Callan stop revealing my secrets."

Brighde started to laugh and changed to a cough. "Since you don't know how to knit, I'm guessing Auntie will be teaching you?"

"Yes, she will," Kayleigh said.

"Prepare yourself. It'll take weeks to knit a scarf," she said.

"How hard can it be?" Kayleigh mocked.

"With Auntie teaching you, she rips out every other row or many rows."

"I do want to learn."

"You will learn. Just cultivate patience."

"Is it easier than planting bluebells?"

"No. It's harder. It takes hours to knit a scarf. Keep

trying. Soon, you will be able to knit while thinking of other things. For now, focus hard on what you're doing."

"One more whiskey before sleeping," Graeme said, opening a new bottle.

"Two men should ask for hospitality tomorrow, Dougal and Roland from Glencoe," said Aiden. "Dougal lost his wife in the massacre. They've been camping in the third cave."

"I'll look out for them," he said.

"Rose, Ian enjoyed your pastries. Roland did, too, I imagine. We saw the crumbs on Ian's face, and he said how much he loved them. You made his favorites."

Rose blushed. "I did. He loves them so much. Apple fritters. He stops by the kitchen to check on dessert every day."

"He checks on Rose." Callan teased her.

"You don't know he does," said Rose.

"I know more than you think I do," said Callan as he winked at her.

Brighde hit his arm. "Stop teasing Rose," she said.

"Thank you, Brighde," Rose said.

"I'm here for you." Brighde put her arm around Rose in support.

"I'm ready for sleep," Graeme said.

"I think the chill has warmed," Kayleigh said, and she went upstairs.

Chapter 7

As promised, Ilsa gave knitting lessons for Kayleigh. The women sat knitting and sewing, with Mairi working on her needlepoint designs.

"Bryan seems interested in Fiona," Ilsa announced.

"The trick will be getting Fiona interested in Bryan," Brighde said.

"Should we be matchmaking?" Kayleigh wondered.

"You had a match made by our parents," Brighde indicated, pointing with her knitting needles.

"Look how it turned out." Kayleigh sighed.

"It hasn't turned out at all," Ilsa said.

"My point exactly," she said. "It doesn't always work and can cause harm."

"You feel harmed?" Ilsa questioned. "If I thought you were harmed, I would say his name here and now."

"I have been hurt by it," she said. "I don't mean to whine about it. It's just a fact."

Aiden knocked and entered the room. "Am I interrupting?"

"Aiden," Ilsa said. "Come in. Come in."

"A welcome visit," she said. "What can we do for you?"

"This will be your scarf," Kayleigh said, holding up a loose ten rows of uneven knitting.

"I'm impressed," Aiden said, eyebrows raised. "Very nice."

"It's the exact shade of your stormy eyes," Kayleigh said.

"His eyes are clear sky blue, not stormy," Mairi said, eyes on her needlepoint.

"She was referring to when I'm emotional. Apparently, my eyes turn color into what she calls the stormy blue of Loch Leven." Aiden informed the women.

"She's poetic about his eyes," Brighde noted. She lost track and had to recount her stitches.

"I noticed one day they change color when he's emotional. We had a discussion about the color of his eyes on patrol last night," Kayleigh said.

"It's still poetic," Ilsa said. "Kayleigh, don't get attached to your knitting. We'll start over when Aiden leaves. The better it would be for him not to hear you cry."

"I don't cry over knitting," Kayleigh said. "I don't cry much at all."

"Then not to hear you fuss," Ilsa corrected. "You do fuss up a storm."

"There's your storm," Mairi noted.

"What can we help you with, Aiden?" Ilsa asked.

"Rose sent me. Would you like refreshments?" he asked.

"Yes, thank you." Ilsa spoke for the group.

When he left the room, she commented on his visit. "His excuse was poor."

"What then did he want?" Mairi asked.

"To spy on us," Kayleigh said.

"To see Kayleigh," Brighde corrected her.

"To check and see what we're doing, and he didn't stop at the doorway until he saw Kayleigh," said Mairi.

"Poor Rose," Brighde sympathized. "She needs to make a tray for us. All at Aiden's request."

"If I were a betting woman, I'd wager he carries the tray," Ilsa said.

"You're right. He wouldn't ask Rose to bring it to us," Kayleigh agreed.

"Prepare yourself, Kayleigh," Ilsa warned her.

"Oh no! Not now. Don't rip it out. Look at this knitting. Sure, it's a perfect sample for a student of knitting. You just want me to be miserable." Kayleigh moaned. "It's a lot better than the past six samples."

Despite her protest, Ilsa proceeded to undo Kayleigh's knitting. "Don't you see each time you get better at it?"

"If you would let me keep the samples, I could see it," Kayleigh declared.

"You'll have to take my word for it," Ilsa stated. "Have you gone to the river yet?"

"No, I haven't thought about it," Kayleigh replied.

"You should take your snacks with Aiden by the river," Brighde disclosed. "Wildflowers and willow trees line its banks. It's very beautiful."

"I'll ask him about it. I didn't think to ask about where we should stop to eat. He's the patrol chief. It hasn't even crossed my mind. I'll ask him tomorrow," Kayleigh said. "I do miss Loch Leven. It will be good to see the river."

Aiden carried in a serving tray.

"Enjoy your snack," he said as he left.

Focused on her knitting, Kayleigh mumbled her thanks.

"We were right," Kayleigh declared. "A break from the knitting is just what we needed."

****

They ate their cheese and bread, gazing into one another's eyes.

As they gathered chestnuts, Aiden sang in his fine baritone voice.

"Here," He patted the blanket by his side. Kaleigh sat, and then they lay side by side. He laid out his arm for her pillow, and she laid her head on his left arm.

"Come closer. I won't take advantage."

She sighed in relief and laid her head on his shoulder. *I think I wouldn't mind if he did.* She didn't know what to do with her hands and shifted herself.

He took her left hand in his right and placed it over his heart. *I feel his heart beating. His breath moves my hair. I love being close to him. He's so warm, body and soul.*

She awakened to the blue of twilight. "Aiden, we slept. It's late."

"Don't worry. I'll marry you. We're already…"

"Already?"

"Half married if Graeme would have his say."

Startled, she sat up. "Can he force us?"

"Would it be forcing us? I'd say we would get along. And there's this attraction between us."

"It's so comfortable."

"Like friends?"

"No. Like more than friends. But there's my handfast. We must remember. Today, I forgot. It's confusing. This attraction is forbidden."

"Forbidden? I am not forbidden anything."

"But I am forbidden anyone except my future husband. And I have my reputation to lose. What if he finds out?" She stood up, her hands shaking.

Aiden stood facing her, hands on his hips. "Maybe he would be happy for us?"

"Are you crazy?"

"No. I just wish things would be different. I wish you would realize…you would love me. If you did, everything would all work out fine."

"You are wishing on rainbows," she said.

"Rainbows symbolize hope. I have hope you will come to love me."

"You are so frustrating!"

By then, they were heading back at a fast pace.

"Other men don't do it."

"What men? Who else are you frustrating?"

"No one. Just you! I mean, you are frustrating me," she said.

"Oh, good. No one else is frustrating you."

"No, it's your privilege."

"As long as it is confined to me." He grabbed her hand, and they broke into a run.

It was dark by the time they reached Callan, who was looking for them.

"You two want a forced handfast? Graeme will not be talked out of it this time. The last time a couple came in this late, they were forced," Callan said.

"They wanted to be handfasted. Don't you remember their blissful faces? Their parents had kept them apart. So Graeme did them a favor," Aiden stated. "It wasn't forced at all."

"Maybe he will do you a favor this time."

"What favor?" Kayleigh queried.

"Handfast," Callan answered.

"But I am already handfasted," she said.

"Indeed, you are," Callan said. "But it can be

broken."

"Handfasts in Caledonia are marriages. In extreme circumstances, they can be broken, like when a man strikes his wife or abuses his children," Aiden explained. "It doesn't matter if the minister has blessed the marriage or not."

"It's not popular with the clergy." Callan clarified the process.

Graeme was waiting for them outside the keep. "First, the kissing tree. Now returning in the night. You two are handfast for a reason."

"We must wait for our betrothed to come to us," Kayleigh replied. "Then we will marry."

"Oh, for goodness sake Aiden. Will you confess now?"

"I already confessed my love for her. She wants to wait—"

"For my future husband to come to me. I don't want to break the handfast," she insisted.

"She doesn't know?" Graeme asked.

"As I told you, I don't know who he is," she said.

"You see?" Aiden stared into Graeme's eyes.

****

Aiden sat close after dinner, hand on her shoulder, fingering her hair. Tendrils of awareness slid across her abdomen. Her heartbeat sped, thumping against her chest. He couldn't know what she was feeling, yet when she looked at his face, a sleepy glint in his eyes said otherwise. She glanced away and then back again to double-check. A tender smile reached his eyes, showing her he had noticed. His arm on her shoulder squeezed her close and released her. She still sat close, enjoying his warmth. *Thank goodness he stopped playing with my hair. I'm flushed. Everyone saw the effect his touch had on me. How embarrassing.*

"Are you feeling well, Kayleigh?" Brighde asked. "You look like you have a fever."

Callan whispered to her.

"Oh. I see," Brighde whispered to him.

"Yes," Mairi, who had overheard, said in a loud whisper.

"They're just now figuring out we have an attraction," said Aiden.

Callan laughed.

Brighde hit his arm. "Stop laughing."

Kayleigh blushed even more and lifted the cup for a drink but did it to hide her face. As the others struggled to hold in laughter, she rested the cup on the table and covered her face with her hands.

Aiden peeled her fingers and hands from her face. "An attraction is a happy thing, nothing to hide from. They are happy to have their suspicions confirmed. Laughter can be the result of happiness."

Though she didn't laugh, a big smile lit her face, and she felt the flush fading.

"Remember, I'm still handfasted and must be true to him. You need to tell me his name so I can discuss this with him," Kayleigh demanded.

"It's okay. We don't need to act on the attraction," he said. "You won't betray him."

"But where's the line of betrayal? How will I know what to do?"

"Guilt," Callan said. "You will know."

"Aiden won't push you to do anything you don't want," Graeme reached for his cup of ale.

"The king with his decree," Callan teased.

"This is serious. Kayleigh is afraid she will do the wrong thing. It's possible to feel guilty when doing nothing wrong," Graeme reminded them.

"And to do something wrong without feeling guilty," Mairi added.

"Kayleigh has a strong moral compass. She will always do the right thing," Aiden stated.

"I am here, everyone. Please talk about me behind my back, not in my face. I'm joking," said Kayleigh. She scooted away from Aiden and leaned her elbows on the table. "I'm happy to hear your faith in me, Aiden." His eyes had returned to resting blue, the color of her mother's quilt. "I believe you would also do the right thing."

"Yes, I would." Aiden declared his support.

Chapter 8

"Aiden, can we eat in a different place this time?" Kayleigh asked, on patrol with him.

"Yes. Don't you like the tree?" he asked.

"Yes, I like the tree just fine."

"Where would you like to eat?"

"By the river. I'm told there's a bench with wildflowers around it. Brighde says it's beautiful." She waved her arms toward the river.

"The river. I don't go to the river."

"Why not?"

"It's where my brother Iain died."

"Are you afraid of the water?"

"No. Who said I was afraid?"

"No one said it. Who would say it?"

"Callan, maybe."

"Brighde spoke to me about it."

"She and Callan spend much time in one another's company."

"No one said you are afraid."

"I'll take you to the river. Do you think they're seeing too much of each other?"

"I'll get Brighde to take me. They're doing well together. They were always paired in Glencoe."

"True. I suppose it's natural."

"I'll go another day with Brighde and Callan."

"No, we'll go today."

"Why do you worry about Brighde and Callan?"

"I don't worry about them. It's just…in Caledonia, Callan has been known as a ladies' man, with more than one lady friend," said Aiden.

"He has? In Glencoe, he was always with Brighde and no one else."

"It can lead to expectations."

"Right. So far, he has only been seen with Brighde since we've been here."

"It warrants attention. We'll watch them, and I'll speak with Graeme if necessary."

"Why talk with Graeme about it?"

"Only if it is necessary. He has a way with people, and Callan listens to him."

"Of course. It makes sense," said Kayleigh.

"The same way it would if you were being difficult and I went to Brighde," said Aiden.

"No. You would talk with me, speak only to me." Kayleigh shook her head. "The things you think are often questionable."

Aiden laughed. "I'm teasing you. I didn't mean it."

"Thank you. I hear the river."

"The rushing water. Let's go now."

****

"Oh, it's beautiful. First, the lavender by the manor. Now, a field of bluebells with a path through it. The sight of it is breathtaking, so much purple! And it makes breathing a pleasure," said Kayleigh. "The willow trees are lovely."

"It is beautiful like you say."

"The river is blue like your eyes, your resting eyes."

"My dear, you haven't seen my resting eyes." He wiggled his eyebrows.

"You're silly."

"Do tell me, Miss Kayleigh, how may I be? What is permissible?"

"Anything is permissible, but I get to complain."

He burst out laughing.

"I didn't mean it like…Men!"

"I can't tease or be permissible," he said.

"I just don't like teasing. You have always been genuine with me. Now you tease me to get a reaction. Why the change?"

"I think it's working together. In Glencoe, we were friends. I oversaw your education. It's confusing. I tell you things I would tell the men, and it changes how I treat you."

"You don't tell them about the water, do you?"

"No."

"You tell me because we are friends, not just a patrol team. Right?"

"Yes, You're right. I'll give it thought."

Kayleigh fell silent.

"Not now," he said. "I'll think about it when I review the day."

"You review the day?"

"Yes, at the end of the day, I have two fingers of whiskey and think about the day and its events. Patrol related and personal."

"Maybe I'll try this. I tend to think all the time about what's happening or being said. Then, at the end of the day, I snuggle with Robbie and enjoy his closeness."

They walked to the river bench and sat. They spread out their food from the basket Rose had left for them.

"Look, Rose tied a purple ribbon on the basket. Be careful we don't lose it."

"You may keep it. It's from my mother's collection of ribbons. When she passed, we left her personal items intact for fear of soiling them."

"But we aren't sure, so I'll save it for Rose. She may want to use it again."

Kayleigh stood to open the basket and distribute the food. She took a single step backward.

"Watch out!" Aiden shouted.

"I'm okay," Kayleigh declared.

"Stay away from the river."

"I'm here. Stop worrying."

"I'm not worrying. You stepped toward the river."

"I took one step."

"I saw two steps."

"I stepped with one foot and brought the other next to it. The result was one step away from the bench."

"I suppose you're right."

"Fine. Now let's eat Rose's delicious meal."

"Mmm…apple turnovers."

"Aha!" She laughed.

"Okay, you were right. They're my favorite." He laughed with her.

"Look, there are Mairi and Graeme on the other side of the river." Kayleigh pointed at them.

"They're on the same side of the river as us. There's a bend in the river. It's a winding river."

"It's Mairi and Graeme walking together."

"So I see."

"You don't think it's odd?"

"They get along together."

"Right!"

"Don't plan any matchmaking. It never ends well. Think of your own—"

"Handfast. Don't worry. Brighde's the matchmaker in my family. It wouldn't surprise me if they are out walking together because she arranged it."

"I think Graeme can arrange his own walks."

"Of course he can."

"He's a grown man, after all, not a boy."

"He must have always seemed grown to you. You admired him as a boy."

"We all did since he was eldest."

"I don't think Brighde admired me."

"Yes, she did. She tried to do everything you did," he said. "I remember she wanted to be an archer."

"Remember when she tried shooting the arrow, sitting on the horse?"

"She scared everyone, even the horse," he said. "Then there was the day I taught you to make a fire, and she followed suit, trying to carry the huge log from the hearth and rolled it on the floor, almost catching fire to the fresh reeds and filling the cottage with smoke."

"Aunt Ilsa came coughing out, dragging Brighde, whose hands were burned. We both had sore bottoms at the end of the day."

"Then all of us had to clean the house and set a new hearth fire."

"Yes," said Kayleigh. "The river is fast."

Aiden shuddered. Memories of Iain being swept away filled his mind.

His eyes fixed on the river. All he could see was Iain, and he felt himself at eight years old, helpless as Graeme rescued Iain, then hopeful as Graeme pulled him out of the water, only then for him to die. His brother had drowned as he stood there watching. If he had tried to rescue him, then he would have died too. At the time, he'd wished he would have died instead of his two-year-old brother. He could lift him on land. He hadn't been able to carry him, though. It hadn't mattered because he hadn't known how to swim.

Until then, only Graeme could swim. His summers had been spent swimming in Caledonia. After Iain's death, they had all taken swim lessons at Loch Leven.

"You're pale. Are you okay?" Kayleigh's concern was clear.

"Yes. I was thinking of Iain."

"You couldn't have saved him. You were only—"

"Eight years old. I know. As an adult, I can look back and see I couldn't have saved him. But I still have an eight-year-old in me who didn't have the skill or strength to rescue a two-year-old."

"It was burned into my brain. It hurts to remember. He was two, and I was eight. A very skinny eight. He fell into the river. I was too weak to try to swim and called for Graeme, who was fourteen. He ran and jumped in to save Iain. But Iain had drowned. If I could have saved him… Graeme fished him out of the water, but we couldn't revive him. I've always blamed myself. I got to the edge of the water and couldn't make myself go into the river."

"You couldn't go in. You would have drowned."

"I could have tried. I might have been able to grab his red tunic. I still see his blonde hair, the color of Callan's hair, against the red tunic. The next spring, we all had swimming lessons."

"Yes, I remember. I just don't remember Iain. I'm sorry."

"Because you never met him. He was too young to visit Glencoe with us. My uncle wouldn't have been able to care for him."

"What about Graeme? He was old enough to come."

"He was being trained to become Chief. Then our parents died."

She nodded yes. "In the carriage accident. We missed you and Callan."

"We missed two years, two Springs. We went to Glencoe the second summer and returned in the fall. Graeme insisted we be allowed to continue the tradition, especially since…the memorable ceremony."

"Oh, you mean my handfast."

If she would just remember. "Yes, your handfast."

"Why won't you tell me who he is?"

"Who he is?"

"Stop." She slapped his shoulder. "You know who he is. Why won't you tell me?"

"It's for him to do."

"But he hasn't come forth."

"Promises were made. All in attendance were sworn to secrecy."

"Why a secret?"

"All the parents wanted you to fall in love with him."

"But if I don't know who he is, how can I fall in love with him?"

"They wanted it to happen naturally."

"There's no reason for you to avoid the river. You're strong now."

"Yes, I've worked hard all my life to be strong, capable, and brave."

"And you are those things."

"But I have not been tested."

"You tell me about the spring games where all the

men are tested. You are the caber toss champion every year."

"Ever since I was seventeen."

"Eight years of being strong, capable, and brave. Your patrolling and being chief of the patrol is brave. Competing in archery against me is brave."

"What?"

She giggled. "Just testing to see if you were paying attention to what I was saying."

When they finished eating, he patted the bench closer to him. She moved next to him and let him take her hand. They sat for a time. He squeezed her hand. She squeezed his. They leaned their heads toward one another.

"We need to go back on patrol," she said.

He let go of her hand and sighed.

"Let's go." He took her hand to help her, but she pulled her hand back.

"All business now. You're correct," he said.

Chapter 9

"Kayleigh!" Brighde said. "Wait for me."

She slowed. It was a common refrain of their childhood. Kayleigh went farther and faster than they were allowed, and Brighde corrected her or called for her to stop.

"We're not supposed to go farther than the third row of pear trees."

"Why? They didn't give a reason. We could push on farther."

"Mark my words, there will be a good reason."

As they passed the sixth row, they heard giggling. They knew it was the sixth because Brighde counted the rows aloud as they passed them.

"Oh, dear," Brighde said.

"Shh…" Kayleigh warned so the couple wouldn't hear them.

They both turned their horses and galloped back to the chestnut trees they had passed next to the pear grove.

"Callan tied a satchel so we can bring chestnuts. He loves them the way you do," Brighde said.

"Hazelnuts, though, are my favorite." Kayleigh began picking chestnuts off the ground.

They dismounted the horses, removed the satchel, and gathered chestnuts until the satchel was full.

"Oh no!" Brighde exclaimed.

"What's wrong?" Kayleigh asked, ready to tie her

satchel on Beauty.

"The horses. Where are the horses?"

"They must have gone home."

"But how did they get loose?"

"Brighde, did you tie your horse?"

"Oh dear. No."

"Me too. We have a long walk back."

"A long walk home," she said.

"Home. Is this home to you now?"

"It's the only home we have."

"True. I wonder when it will begin to feel like home."

"The moment Graeme welcomed us."

"What if my own true love died at Glencoe or ran off to join his family?"

"He will come for you."

"How can you know this?"

"Callan assured me he will come for you."

"Of course, he knows. How does he know?"

"He was at the handfast."

"Of course. He was sworn—"

"To secrecy."

"If you remember who it is, will you tell me?"

"No. If I remember who it is, then I, too, will be sworn to secrecy."

"A three-year-old sworn to secrecy?"

"No. A nineteen-year-old who remembers is sworn to secrecy."

"By this rule, I would be sworn to secrecy when I remember."

"You're right! It means he would need to tell you first before you remember."

"Oh no. It will never happen!"

"I'm teasing you, Kayleigh. When you remember, if you remember, then tell me. We will hunt him and force him to marry you."

"Stop! This is a serious matter to me."

"I apologize, dear. I'll stop."

"Let's just walk and not talk."

"Walk and not talk? Am I hearing right?" Aiden's deep voice startled them.

"Not possible," Callan said. "This can't be anyone we know."

"It's us!" Brighde answered.

They ran to the men who were riding horses.

"I can't believe we didn't hear you," Kayleigh said.

"We heard your voices above the horses' hooves," Callan said.

"No, we didn't," Aiden said. "We almost collided with the women before we heard them because the wind is blowing through the chestnut trees."

"Did you get the chestnuts?" Callan asked.

"Yes, we have them," Brighde said as she gave him the full bag. She and Kayleigh had taken turns carrying it.

The men helped them onto the saddles in front of them. Kayleigh liked the warmth of Aiden's hand on her stomach, holding her against him. He hugged her tight and then held her with a firm hand. She melted back against him.

"We worried when the horses returned without you," he said, coughing to clear his throat.

"We worried when they left. We were picking chestnuts when the horses sneaked off without us. They could use training," Kayleigh noted.

"It's always the humans who require training to

interact with animals." Callan directed them toward home.

Kayleigh enjoyed the warmth of Aiden wrapped around her. *What would it be like to have him wrapped around me all night long? He would have to be the one handfasted to me. But would he? I prefer him to others, though I don't meet many others. But he is fine and glorious. And sweet and kind.*

"What possessed you to go get chestnuts so late in the day?" Aiden queried.

"We thought—" said Kayleigh.

"You thought. Did you discuss this with anyone prior to going? No. Oh, excuse me, you discussed it with each other. Know this and hear me well. You need permission to go out on the horses."

"We had permission."

"Of course, Callan or Bryan let you take the horses, but you didn't tell them where you were going, did you? No. I know this because no one in their right mind would have let you go at this hour, unescorted."

"You are not kind after all and have a bitter quality I hadn't noticed before," Kayleigh noted.

"Who said I am kind?"

"No one. It was a fleeting thought. I must have seen you be kind and thought it a character trait."

"Was anything I said untrue?"

"No. You are honest to a fault. I just don't want to hear it."

"You are in no position not to hear it."

"We do not need to be scolded like children."

"Why did you go so far?"

"Callan mentioned he likes chestnuts, and we thought to pick them for him."

"I knew he would be involved. Callan, think before you speak."

"I could say the same to you right now," he said with irritation. "You are being rude. Did you not think they were afraid when the horses left them? It's a good thing they stayed on the path, or they might have gotten themselves lost. You scolding them doesn't help. Kayleigh is trapped on Star with you, and it is unfair to treat her like this."

"No, I hadn't thought of it. Ilsa and Graeme will be waiting for us outside. I'll allow them to further scold you when we return."

"Hmph," Kayleigh mumbled.

Chapter 10

Beauty had taken a liking to Kayleigh soon after she had arrived from Glencoe. She waited for Kayleigh in the paddock each afternoon following her patrol shift, saddled and ready to ride. She seemed to like it best when she was given control of where to go, with limits. She and Aiden rode side by side to go practice archery.

"Tell me what you remember about your handfast," Aiden said as they started toward the archery field.

"It's hard to tell the difference between what is memory and what I've been told. I remember the boy being older. I'm told he was nine years old. He was kind and said he liked me. He said he chose me when his father asked who he would marry. I just can't remember his name. He had long black hair, like yours, and blue eyes. Yours is thick. He reminds me of you. But I know it isn't right because it would have been revealed to me many years ago. Ilsa or Brighde, or even Callan would have told me. They were all there. Were you there, Aiden?"

"I was…there. I know him, though I am sworn to secrecy."

"Why secrecy? Why would they do it to me?"

"Your parents wanted you to fall in love like they did. They were a true match, your parents. I remember it."

"How can I fall in love if I don't even know who he

is?"

"If I could tell you, then I would."

"Have I met him yet?"

"Yes."

"At the handfasting, I suppose."

"Yes, but after it too. It's all I can say," he said. "If I said more, then you would know him, and I would be breaking the vow. Let me ask you another question. Would you ever consider marrying me?"

"But I'm handfasted."

"I know. But if you weren't handfasted, would you consider me?"

"I feel disloyal even thinking about it, but yes, I suppose I'd consider you."

"Thank you, Kayleigh. I don't know if I feel better or worse now."

"You know I can't even think of marrying you. It would be too sad to want it when I can't do it."

"Change in subject."

"Okay."

"What's your plan for today?"

"Practice archery on horseback."

"I know, but how?"

"Trotting, cantering, and galloping."

"First accuracy, then for speed?"

"Of course."

They galloped away toward the targets Callan had placed in the field for the event. He would also retrieve the arrows Kayleigh shot from horseback. Aiden's whistle would signal when she would begin.

When the whistle blew, she gave Beauty a gentle kick. As they trotted past the target, Kayleigh let an arrow fly. She hit the target at the edge. She tried five times before she hit the center. Then they sped. Cantering from a distance, as they approached the target, she sent an arrow speeding to the target. She couldn't see the target until they turned around. Looked like it was close. Yes, it missed the center by a hair. After two more tries, the arrow hit the center. Next try was at a gallop. She hit center on the first try and the next set.

They were heading back to the stables when an arrow flew past Kayleigh. She turned toward where the arrow had been shot. She and Aiden found Fiona standing by the trees, shaking like a willow tree. She didn't have a bow or arrows.

"Who shot the arrow?" Aiden angrily demanded an answer.

"Not me. I didn't do it," Fiona defended herself.

"You saw who did it." Kayleigh accused her.

"No, I didn't. I was watching you," Fiona said.

"It happened beside or in front of you." Aiden indicated the hole in her story.

"So you saw it," Kayleigh said.

Fiona cried.

"Who did it, Fiona?" Aiden demanded, raising his fist.

"You're going to make her cry more," Kayleigh warned.

"You think I care?" he asked.

Fiona cried harder.

"Fiona, we know you didn't do anything wrong," Kayleigh said to appease her. "Nothing will happen to you."

"He said he would kill me. He had a big knife," Fiona said, face pale and sickly looking.

"So you didn't call out a warning?" Kayleigh noted.

"Even though he had to drop the knife to shoot the arrow," Aiden added.

"I didn't think of that," Kayleigh said.

"But he could have shot me with the arrow," Fiona whined.

"Better he shoot Kayleigh than to shoot you?" Aiden asked.

"Yes. You would have done the same thing," Fiona accused.

"If you think this, then you don't know me. I'd take the shot for Kayleigh every time," he said.

"It was a man," Fiona described him. "A big man I never saw before."

"What is his name?" Kayleigh hoped for a specific answer.

"I don't know. I said I don't know him." Fiona sounded terrified. "He said he would kill me. He means it. He said he tried to shoot you one other time. He said he would kill you or me today. Since he didn't kill you, he'll kill me!"

"Return to the stables with Kayleigh. You can ride with her," Aiden ordered.

"No. Beauty won't take her, not after Fiona kicked her," Kayleigh reported.

"You kicked a horse?" Aiden said. "I believe Kayleigh, so tell the truth."

"Yes. I was scared. The horse jumped at me," Fiona said.

"Because first, you kicked me. Beauty was protecting me, and I let her scare you," Kayleigh said. "She knows you don't like me. She knows you would have let me be killed."

"How does she know?" Fiona asked.

"Her horse sense told her. She is here where she can see, hear, and feel everything," Kayleigh said.

"Kayleigh believes horses are smarter than we are," Aiden said.

"They are smarter than all human beings," Kayleigh told Fiona.

"Even smarter than Aiden?" Fiona sounded worried.

"Yes, smarter than everyone," Kayleigh confirmed.

Fiona gasped.

"You need to ride with me," Aiden said.

"Just give her what she wants, why don't you?" Kayleigh said.

"Then you would be dead," Aiden said.

"More of the same," Kayleigh said.

Fiona giggled.

"What are you doing?" Aiden asked.

"Getting up behind you," Fiona said, right foot in the left stirrup.

"Get off," Aiden demanded. After she did, he dismounted, hoisted her into the saddle, and mounted behind her. "Now sit still, or you'll be thrown to the ground."

To his amazement, she did not bounce in the saddle. *This one knew horses. Why pretend she doesn't? Or is she shaken?*

"Think you're slick, do you? You know horses. Any more tricks like this, and I'll let the man kill you," said Aiden. His voice reached Kayleigh and Beauty, who were in front of them.

"I was right! She feigns fear," Kayleigh whispered.

"I think she was terrified of the man, though," Aiden said.

"I was," Fiona said, her voice trembling.

"I'll see you at the stables," Kayleigh called as she shot forward. "Let's go, Beauty!"

While Bryan cooled Beauty at the stables, Kayleigh watched from indoors, anxious for Aiden to return. *Where is he? No doubt delivering Fiona safe at home. And to be alone to scold me for leaving safety, as if he could stop an arrow. Oh right. He stopped the arrow last time. Glad it didn't hit Beauty or either of us this time. Fiona is the second person to see this man who tried to kill me. Who is it? I haven't offended anyone except Fiona. This man is angry, wanting to kill me. What did I do? How can we stop him? I can't stay in the manor all the time. Anyone near me is in danger. Aiden's not going to let me patrol with him. I'll have to stay inside for protection.*

"Kayleigh! Are you here?" Aiden called to her.

There he is.

"Where's Kayleigh? Bryan, did Kayleigh return?" Aiden sounded worried.

"I'm right here," she said and left the stables. "Bryan made me stay inside. You'll see him with Beauty. I rode her too hard."

"Why?" he said.

"I don't know. I was scared. And don't ask why."

"It's reasonable. You were almost killed."

"I wasn't—"

"You were. A few seconds later, and it would have hit you."

"But he was off by several yards."

"Timing is everything. You know this."

"Okay. He was several seconds off. Do you think he is the same man—"

"Who shot at you the first time? Yes. I have a

description from Fiona. He is about Callan's height. He has a paunchy little belly, her words, not mine, has disheveled red hair, and a bulbous red nose with red lines on it. He has black eyes, or maybe his eyes are very dilated."

"It doesn't sound like anyone I know."

"Both descriptions include the nose with lines on it, and the red hair. It's the same man."

"Yes. How do we capture him? We need a plan," Kayleigh stated.

"No. No plan until I meet with Callan and Graeme. You're not going on patrol until we capture him," Aiden said.

****

They discussed it after dinner.

"The description is the same," Aiden said, "so we're sure it's the same man."

"Fiona's description was more detailed," Graeme noted.

"Of course it was," Kayleigh added. "She was face to face with him threatening her life," said Kayleigh.

"No one ever accused Fiona of being brave," Callan interjected his wit.

"Do you think she's feeding him information?" Graeme sipped from his cup of ale.

"I hadn't thought so," Kayleigh leaned both arms on the table and nibbled at her apple tart.

"She would do it to hurt Kayleigh," Brighde insisted.

"If he threatens her life, she'll do as he wants," Aiden said.

"And he already did," Callan said. "So she's still giving him information."

"Kayleigh will have to avoid patrolling tomorrow," Graeme said.

Kayleigh groaned her disappointment.

"Agreed," Aiden rubbed her back and lightly squeezed the back of her neck. "Sorry, love."

"Agreed. Sorry Kayleigh," Callan sympathized. "It's a matter of your safety."

"I agree, though I don't seem to have a vote, even though you are my sister." Brighde said. "I'm sorry dear."

"Since I don't have a death wish, I will agree," Kayleigh said, "though I reserve the right to act at will if threatened."

"You agree to do as you're told?" Brighde asked, surprised she had changed her mind.

"No. I agree. I'll not patrol tomorrow," Kayleigh corrected their assumption.

"You need to agree to the entire plan," Aiden demanded as he turned toward her.

"Assuming you share the plan with me," Kayleigh said. "I simply can't agree to a plan I don't know."

"Fair enough," Graeme said. As he put his empty cup down, he slammed it on the table, making Brighde and Kayleigh cringe.

"Oh no, here it comes." Callan indicated. He held his cup lifting it in her direction. "I salute you Miss Kayleigh."

Kayleigh grinned and winked at Callan, twirling a strand of her hair.

"That action may have worked when we were children, Kayleigh, but we have long been wise to your attempts at diversion." Aiden stood, hands flat on the table as he looked at them. "She's going to try to negotiate the plan."

"There will be no negotiations, Kayleigh." Graeme stood and frowned at her. He was a very large man. Aiden had been the tallest man at Glencoe. Graeme was a hand's length taller.

Callan laughed and remained seated, relaxing his legs.

Brighde copied his posing.

Kayleigh remained seated, knowing she would do what would be necessary. How odd it was that Aiden and Graeme felt they had to stand. "I will negotiate if my life is at risk."

"Okay," Graeme said, apparently thinking he had resolved the issue.

Aiden groaned.

Chapter 11

Fiona met Kayleigh on the path leading to the house.
"I want to talk to you," she said.
"What do you want? Go ahead and speak to me," Kayleigh replied.
"Come home with me," Fiona said. "I need your help."
"What could you need from me?"
"Um…well…uh…"
"The man is there, isn't he? You want me to walk in there and give myself to him."
"He's going to kill me."
"Then go tell Aiden where he is."
Fiona turned and ran toward home.
Kayleigh yelled, "Aiden!"
"I'm right here," Aiden said. He held her close for a few seconds.
"Fiona was here trying to get me to go with her. The man is at her cabin! She tried to get me to go there."
"Kayleigh, what's wrong?" Brighde asked.
"Graeme!" Aiden yelled as he ran to Fiona's cabin.
Graeme ran to him.
Kayleigh and Brighde watched them reach the door and force it open.
Fiona came out, trying to get the men to stay out. They went in for a moment and returned outside, shaking their heads. They went behind the cabin and into the

brush. They returned empty-handed.

"You were right," Aiden said. "We found big boot prints inside her back window. He must have used the window. There were no other footprints."

"We need to set guard around Fiona," Graeme said.

"But it's Kayleigh he is trying to kill," Brighde reasoned.

"If we guard the front and back of her cabin, he won't be able to get her to help him," Aiden said. "And we need a guard to follow her wherever she goes."

"We need four armed men. Two to follow her," Graeme said.

"Who will guard Kayleigh?" Brighde wrung her hands together.

"Ian will guard her. He'll not get past him," Aiden said. "And he is loyal, a close cousin."

"Why not you or Graeme?" Kayleigh wondered.

"We'll take the morning shift," he said. "This way we can cover the manor tomorrow. Ian will cover the Hall tonight. We'll put two guards to cover the outdoors."

"The great hall is finished for tonight, except for guards and patrol." Graeme noted. "But they'll be leaving soon, and it will be empty."

"I see. So any interruption will be seen as threatening," Kayleigh explained. "It's a good plan. I'll cooperate. Where will I be?"

"In bed," Ilsa rubbed her back.

"How can I sleep while all this is happening?" Kayleigh felt uncomfortable not being the person in control of a situation.

"What is happening?" Aiden said. "Everything will be quiet. Ian will be on guard duty."

****

A loud crash awakened Kayleigh. *What is wrong with Robbie?* "Robbie. Come here." She patted the bed. "What's the matter, baby? It's the middle of the night." He hit her hand with his paw, nails sticking her. "Ow! That's bad." He never used nails with her.

Kayleigh awakened fully to the putrid smell of a man. He was in her room. Fear paralyzed her. *Aiden, help me.* She couldn't speak. It was like her worst nightmare, where she screamed for help, but no sound came out. *Maybe it is a nightmare.* She pinched herself hard and felt pain. *Not a nightmare. Real life. What should I do? Aiden's advice when I was sixteen...get angry. I am strong.* An arm came over her face. Hairs tickled her nose, and she sneezed. "Shut up bitch. By morning I will have you. You will be mine."

She struggled to no avail and thought to distract him. She pulled him close to lift her knee to his groin and instead became tangled in her nightgown.

"Why are you doing this?"

"Shut up, Kayleigh."

His voice was familiar, but she couldn't place it, except it was a Glencoe voice. Dougal or Roland? She tried to roll over, but again, her long nightgown restricted her.

She felt a cloth over her face.

He lifted her, and she thought she might vomit. She tried to move and couldn't. *The smell...*

****

Aiden awakened for his shift. *There's noise at my door. Odd.* He rose and opened the door. A cat ran into the room and dashed from the bed to the window to his dresser. And did the rotation two more times. The cat was distraught. "What's wrong, Robbie? Did you bother Kayleigh so much she let you out?" He tried to pet him and was swatted with what felt like needles scraping his skin. "Ouch. You ratty cat. Are you hungry? Let's get you food." He pulled on his trews and a shirt and went downstairs to see Rose.

She was preparing to cook. Robbie had followed Aiden downstairs. "Morning, Rose," he said.

"Good morning, Aiden. I see his feline lordship followed you. He's been full of vinegar today. Near tore apart my kitchen. The flour turned over, eggs broken. He stopped to sniff the bacon and take a lick. Then the varmint started again. You'd think Kayleigh would be looking for him by now."

Brighde entered the kitchen. "What's happening in here? Is Robbie crazy hungry?"

"Crazy, yes. Hungry, no," Rose said. "See the plate of cheese bits? He won't eat it."

"He's never refused cheese before. Where's Kayleigh?"

"You'd think he would awaken her. She must be in a deep sleep," Aiden said.

They all looked at the kitchen entrance as if expecting Kayleigh to appear.

Robbie yowled. And yowled again, tail twitching fast.

"I'm going to check on Kayleigh." Aiden said. "She's the person who can settle him."

Brighde corrected him. "No, I'll check on her. You would startle her. Then she would awaken in a bad mood."

Brighde went upstairs and returned with the news Kayleigh was already awake but not in her room.

"Rose, have you seen Ian yet, or Kayleigh?" Aiden asked.

"No," said Rose. "It's odd because I expect him to be picking at the sweets."

"I expect to see him before breakfast," he said.

"Where do you think he is?" Brighde wondered.

"He must have heard us," Aiden added.

"Then he left?" Rose asked. "Surely he would wish us good morning?"

"It's not like him. He is a guard and a good one," Aiden said. "He would follow protocol and give report before leaving."

"Maybe he saw the man and gave chase."

"He wouldn't leave his post for a distraction."

"What's this over here? These dark spots." Brighde pointed to the floor.

"It looks like blood. Go now, find Graeme," Aiden ordered.

He went into the parlor and found Ian unconscious with an arrow through his shoulder. It had just missed his neck. "Ian!" He tried to shake him awake without success. "Sorry old fellow, but this will hurt." He moved the arrow. Ian groaned and awakened.

"What happened?" Aiden queried.

"What do you think happened?" Ian said. "By the time I saw him at the entrance, he shot me. Lucky shot. He must have moved me in here to gain a few extra moments."

"Kayleigh, isn't in her room. He must have taken her." Aiden left the room to search outside.

"Graeme! Callan! Bryan!" Aiden yelled.

Graeme and Callan came running to Aiden. Brighde ran outside.

Mairi arrived behind him too.

"Kayleigh is gone!" said Aiden. "Where's Ilsa?"

"She's with Bryan and Ian. They'll take care of him," Graeme assured him. "There's another guard with them to help lift Ian."

"We need a plan," said Graeme. "Call the guards!"

"Here's my whistle, Brighde. Three short, three long, three short."

Aiden swiftly gave orders. "Graeme, you stay and assign the guards, one group to the stables and beyond, a second to the river, the third straight through the woods to the orchards. My group will take the caves. Callan, you're with me and Bryan. The first two guards go with us to the caves."

"Here comes Beauty without Kayleigh," Callan said. "From the direction of the orchards."

"It's a distraction. The horse tracks head in the direction of the caves but don't return," Aiden argued. "So we go to the caves."

"Let's go now," Callan said. "We'll take Beauty with us. I'll ride her. You ride Star."

They ran to the stables with Beauty. Aiden saddled and mounted Star. Callan mounted Beauty after retrieving his revolver from the stables. They galloped to find the horse tracks and followed them at a walk so they wouldn't lose the trail. Bryan met them on horseback.

Chapter 12

Kayleigh awakened to the sound of water dripping and the sulfur smell of damp cave. The cold seeped into her skin. Her feet felt frozen.

Which cave is this? Help me. She tried to sit. *Dammit, my hands are tied.* She opened her eyes to see a blurry Fiona leaning over her. "It's no use trying to escape," she said.

"You helped him?" Kayleigh's voice barely uttered a sound, for her mouth was tied with a gag.

If I can find a sharp surface. If I could just sit. She tried again but was still too groggy to summon the energy. Her mouth was dry, tied with a cloth. *Anger. Need more anger.*

"Oh, no. He's here." Fiona scooted back, away from Kayleigh.

Boots on the cave floor echoed as the man approached.

"Feeling better?"

His voice was cheery.

It was sickening.

"Oh, you are gagged, are you not?" He gave a happy smile. "Today, you will be mine."

She shivered, nauseous.

He removed the gag and put his flask to her mouth. "Don't be thinking I'll remove the tie around your wrists. Today we'll be wed, and you will thank me properly."

She retched. *Throat so sore. Can't yell like this.* Her spirits took a dive even deeper.

"Here's more ale."

It dribbled on her chin. "No wasting ale," he growled.

"Your aim was off, Doug." she rasped.

"Dougal. Still, don't waste it. Here's more."

She drank fast to revive herself. She coughed so he would give her more.

"Greedy, aren't you? We'll see if it's the same for other appetites. Aiden doesn't deserve you. He let my Maggie die in the cold snow. She could have been safe in the cave with you."

"As I recall, Doug, you didn't believe Aiden's warning and wouldn't let Maggie leave with the other women. We welcomed her. She said you wouldn't let her go. Marrying you is what killed her."

Her head snapped back as he punched her.

"Dammit!" She spit out blood. "Can I have a blanket? It's freezing in here."

"Fiona, tend to my future bride," he said.

Fiona moved forward and wrapped a blanket around her.

Kayleigh wiggled her shoulders so it would fall off.

"Be still," Fiona whispered.

"I need my hands to hold it on."

He glared as if he suspected her plan. "You're too drugged to fight. I did a good job of it."

Fiona untied her hands. "It'll be okay. Bryan and Aiden will find us."

"Hey, quiet over there!"

"It's a good thing I didn't kill you after all, Kayleigh. The kid near killed Aiden. You'll not marry him. You'll marry me. No more wearing pants for you, girl."

"Thank you, Fiona." She rubbed her hands together even though they burned. "Where will we be married, Dougal?" She struggled not to cringe at the thought.

"At your Glencoe cave where Maggie should've been. Where you wouldn't let her be during the evil Campbell attack."

"Where were you during the attack?"

"Was in my home waiting for the Campbells after Maggie ran outside. I didn't want them to hurt her."

"Why didn't you go after her?"

"And freeze in the blizzard?"

"The blizzard had ended."

"She was in the cave with you. Don't ask stupid questions."

"She wasn't in the cave, Dougal. You wouldn't let her go."

He's lost his mind. Desperation filled her.

"Where's Beauty?"

"Don't worry, she'll go home from the orchards and mislead the search party," Dougal said. "Her tracks leading to the cave were wiped and hidden, if Fiona did her job right."

"Beauty will go home," Kayleigh replied.

"To the stables. It will delay the search."

"She's trained to go to the house when she loses me."

He kicked dirt at her.

"You're kicking dirt at me? Such a man."

He aimed to kick her ribs instead but stopped without contact.

"This will teach you," he said.

"Kicking a woman?" she said.

He lifted her and punched her in the face. "Even you can be trained."

She held back her retching. She wouldn't give him the satisfaction of a reaction or another reason to beat her. She stayed silent.

"There. Nothing to say?"

She glared at him.

"Be careful lest I wipe your glare off your face."

He threw a wet cloth at her. "Wipe the dirt off your face."

She was too weak to reach for the cloth.

"Never mind. Fiona, make yourself useful."

Fiona wiped her face with a surprisingly gentle touch. "They'll come for us," she whispered.

"Sss hurts," said Kayleigh. She now noticed Fiona's bruised cheek.

"You should have kept your mouth shut," Fiona reminded her.

Kayleigh tried to shake her head no, and nausea hit her with the dizziness. She saw spots of light.

"Sorry," Fiona said.

"You're not supposed to be talking," Dougal warned. "Unless you want more beauty marks put on your face."

Fiona wiped her own face. "Ow." She ducked as if expecting to be hit.

"Kayleigh, prepare to become my wife." Dougal grinned at her, seemingly delighted.

"But you're already married." Kayleigh tried to argue with him. *Silence be damned!.*

"No, Maggie died in the massacre. You didn't save her," he said. "You hid all those women but not my

Maggie."

"You wouldn't let her come to the cave with me. It's your fault," Kayleigh said. The more they pushed him, the more likely he would make a mistake.

"I thought you wanted me as your wife," Fiona said.

"You want to be his wife?" Kayleigh said in surprise.

"You want to be my wife?" said Dougal. "No matter. Kayleigh's to blame, so she pays the price."

"But she has Aiden. They're in love," Fiona argued, apparently trying to distract him.

"Cease your words, girl!" He walked over and backhanded her in the face.

"Hitting is not the way to get what you want," Kayleigh said. "Fine, I'll marry you."

Fiona looked at her in surprise, then in understanding.

"Stop your lying." His face grew more distorted by the anger.

"I'm not lying. If you stop hitting, I'll marry you," she said.

"Me too. You can have your pick," Fiona said.

"I'll have both of you if I want," he said as he left the cave.

Kayleigh gagged and saw Fiona do the same. It convinced her of Fiona's innocence in the kidnapping.

Kayleigh's stomach and face hurt. She tightened one arm, then the next, then each leg, her stomach, and her back. It helped her circulation, though she had to grit her teeth to do it. She did the strengthening exercises until she could stand straight. Her strength had increased a bit, giving her a sliver of hope to attempt an escape.

Fiona copied her movements. "He brought me here

and tied me up until he came in with you. He's evil."

"And crazed," Kayleigh agreed.

Kayleigh heard boot steps approaching and hurried to sit by the dwindling fire, trying again to appear weak. She grabbed Fiona and pulled her down to sit by her. Elbows on her knees, she bowed her head in defeat and peeked at him. He carried a few logs, put them by the fire, and went out. He returned with more logs. He dropped them on the fire, making sparks fly. "Feeling better yet?"

Kayleigh groaned and touched her bruised face. "No."

"You will. Heat the broth."

"When the fire is ready. Need to stoke it." She pulled a small log off the fire and arranged the two left on the fire. She then put the third on top to draw the fire upward.

Fiona stood up and pushed the other three logs, medium-sized branches, toward her.

Kayleigh tested their weight and chose her weapon.

As she sat there with the blanket around her, she tightened her muscles, focusing on her shoulders, back, and arms. By the time the fire caught, she would be ready.

"What would Maggie think?" Kayleigh wondered aloud.

"She's dead, so she ain't thinking much of anything now," Dougal said. "Ye killed her, not taking her to Coire Gabhail."

"I offered, and you wouldn't let her go."

"I loved my Maggie!"

"Of course you loved her. She was your wife."

He pushed her back onto the ground.

"Maybe I should have a little fun with you," he said. "Nay, you wear pants."

Fiona stepped between them.

Kayleigh's hope dwindled when he moved the three logs away from her. At least the logs remained in the cave. "I'd like to lie down. May I have a log for my headrest?"

He grunted and gave Fiona her chosen log. She put it beneath Kayleigh's head.

Kayleigh lay with her head on the log and almost smiled when Fiona gave her a wink.

"No funny business," he said. "You're too weak to try an escape."

She mumbled and waited, alert to every move he made.

It seemed hours passed with him watching them. He stood and stretched, seemed to doze off a time or two. But when one of them moved to stand, he would awaken. Fiona stoked the fire several times as they hoped for rescue. When light began to enter the cave, the rising sun gave them hope. Now her absence would have been detected. That meant an hour or two of a hard ride if Aiden found the horse trail to the caves. Fiona wouldn't have erased all trace of the trail.

They smiled at each other when the light seemed to brighten at the entrance. Dougal was digging around in his knapsack when Kayleigh decided to attack.

She rose, silent, and lifted her log. She approached him, glad she had no shoes to make a sound. Her heart stopped as he paused and then resumed unpacking. She took care to make no shadows on the wall of the cave. He startled anyway and began to turn as she lifted the log high and smashed it on his head. He fell slumped over his pack. She ran, cold bare feet unstable. She slowed just a bit to gain more traction. She heard Fiona behind her. She sniffled, trying to hold in the cries, but sound escaped her mouth. Heart racing, she longed for Aiden. *Aiden, Aiden. Aiden, Aiden. He will come.*

Fiona and Kayleigh limped out of the entrance as Aiden came running. Callan and two guards ran past them. Bryan lifted Fiona, who sobbed on him.

Aiden grabbed and hugged Kayleigh.

"I thought you were gone. I thought he killed you."

Bruised and beaten, she looked at him.

"I'm sorry," he said, "I wasn't thinking."

Cradling her close, he kissed her forehead opposite the bruise and gave her lips a gentle kiss, and then a firm passionate kiss. He squeezed her shoulders.

She relished all of it. His touch lifted her spirits, even though it hurt. Her heart warmed.

"I think I killed him," she said.

Callan came out to report. "He lives, though he's sore and bloody. She clocked him on the side of the head with a log."

"What if you had missed, if he had turned around?" said Aiden.

"It's okay. I'm okay," she said.

"What's Fiona doing here? An accomplice?"

"I don't know...she helped me...I clobbered him. She distracted him one time, bending low." She winced in pain. "Can we stop talking? It hurts."

"Yes, just be silent if you want. We'll do the talking."

"You should have seen her, Aiden!" Fiona said. "She kicked him in the..." When she looked at Kayleigh, she stopped. "In his nether region. She kicked him, brought him to his knees. I didn't have a weapon in hand the way she did when she hit him over the head. She sure smacked him with the log! Wow, you should have seen her. She's a hero."

"You helped her out of the cave," Bryan said. "You're a hero too." He lifted her onto his horse and mounted it behind her.

"I was just sitting there watching her. She had to make me stand. Then she leaned on me. After she hit him with the log, I gave him a swift kick in the…um…rear. A good, hard kick in the rear. Didn't I, Kayleigh?"

"Yes…you did."

"Brace yourself. I'll mount Star," Aiden directed. "Then Callan and Bryan will hand you to me. It will hurt. Do you want to sit or have me hold you?"

"I'll sit. Thanks." They placed her in the saddle in front of Aiden.

"Poor thing hurts something fierce," Fiona said. "She got hit more than me. She wouldn't be quiet. I was quiet. Wasn't I, Kayleigh? You need to tell them, 'cause they won't believe me otherwise. Right, Kayleigh?" said Fiona.

"Right," said Kayleigh.

"He got me there by telling me she was hurt. But she wasn't there yet. I was too scared to run away. He said he would kill me if I didn't do what he said. So I stayed there. Then Kayleigh came in. She was dropped in and hit her head on the floor. I tried to cushion her, but I was too far away. The son of a… You can see she hurts. Right? Right, Kayleigh?"

"Yes, Fiona."

"You hurt bad? Look at her face. He punched her more than one time. It's a blur. I can't remember everything."

"Probably out of breath," Callan commented.

"Callan," Bryan said.

"It's okay. He's just Callan. He always has something acerbic to say. So says Brighde," Fiona said. "He talks as much as me. It's why I understand him. But I'm nicer. Right, Kayleigh? I can be very nice. Right?"

"Yes." Her response was terse this time.

"Okay, Fiona. Let Kayleigh rest," said Bryan.

They slowed to position behind Aiden and Callan.

Aiden trotted Star a bit until Kayleigh's groans protested. Then he resumed a walk. Star stepped with care.

****

They arrived home to see Brighde running toward them. After Kayleigh was off of Star, Brighde, and Mairi helped her walk inside.

After her visit to the infirmary with Ilsa and Brighde, Aiden placed Kayleigh in her bed, and Ilsa propped her with pillows. Robbie opened one eye, then leaped to lay by Kayleigh's pillow. His presence and loud purring helped calm her.

"I'll get Rose's stew for her and a warm cup of whiskey. You ask questions," said Aiden.

"I'll find out," Ilsa promised.

And he left.

Ilsa brushed out Kayleigh's hair. "Here, let me wash your face, dear."

"Okay." She hated how weak her voice sounded.

"I'm so glad you're okay, dear," Brighde soothed her sister.

"Okay?" Kayleigh asked.

"Okay, as in you're alive," she corrected herself. "I

worried so, feared we would lose you."

"You look so sad. You must hurt terribly," Mairi said as she moved to touch Kayleigh, but Brighde stopped her.

"Yes. How do we make it stop hurting?" Kayleigh asked.

"We bathe you and put you to sleep," Ilsa said.

"It hurts."

"Did you tell the men what happened?"

"No. Not necessary. Fiona told them everything in great detail."

"Chatter?"

"Right. She talked so much and asked me to verify everything she said."

"Oh dear," said Brighde.

"Bryan had to move his horse back, so Fiona couldn't talk to me. But she still chattered away, though I couldn't hear what she said."

"She'll be your new best friend," said Ilsa.

"I did tell the men she helped me. Dougal kidnapped us."

"The one who was married to Maggie?"

"Yes. He's lost his mind. Blames me for her death. Therefore, I should marry him." Kayleigh said.

Brighde held a pan in time for Kayleigh to retch into it. She rinsed out her mouth with water.

"I don't know what is more nauseating, the thought of him or the pain," said Kayleigh.

"I'm sorry you are going through this, dear," Brighde said.

"I wonder if my ribs are broken?"

"They are bruised but not broken," Ilsa said.

I can see your face has been punched," Brighde

commented.

"Twice."

"Did he harm you in any other way?" Ilsa asked.

"He tried, but I kicked him in the…nether region, as Fiona said. He leaned over me. Who knows? Was it his intention? I don't know. But he never got close again."

"Oh dear, thank goodness," Brighde said, folding her hands together.

"Fiona could have made her escape then, but she didn't even try. Not even when I told her to go."

"She was probably stunned by you kicking him."

"She called me a hero when I clobbered him over the head with a log."

"Because you are a hero," Brighde said.

"I was terrified."

"But you behaved with courage. It's what makes you a hero," Ilsa pronounced with hands on her hips.

****

Kayleigh awakened to find Robbie sleeping by her head. He usually slept by her torso, and she cuddled him. This time it seemed he was cuddling her. Her splitting headache was from the injury she'd suffered when falling back to the ground, hitting her head during the kidnapping. She felt bruised and battered. Then she remembered when Leah had been beaten by her husband in Glencoe. She had been black and purple on her face and extremities. Even touching her hand had hurt her. It had taken months for her to heal inside. *I wonder what I look like.*

The uneasy feeling in her stomach made her want to hide under the quilt and imagine her mother's protection. Being in her mother's arms had made her feel safe. She had been three years old and very ill. She still remembered the contented feeling of being in her arms. She was beside herself when her mother died after the handfast.

Would she ever feel safe again? Would she always dread the company of men? Even the thought of Aiden made her feel ill. And he had represented safety to her ever since he was nine years old.

She suddenly remembered all of it. The handfast had been held outdoors, and their hands had been tied together. They held hands which were bound by a strip of MacDonald tartan. They said words. She supposed they had been vows. Two children making adult vows. What had they been thinking? The adults should have known better. She had been fierce, wild, even then. Aiden, her friend, her champion, her safe place, had been her husband all along. All these years, a secret kept from her. No matter their vow of silence about the handfast. She had found out about the vow when she became of marriageable age. Then she fell victim to Blake, who used her to get to Brighde. When Aiden found out about him, he had been so angry. Of course, he had. Thinking about his wife under the influence of another man must have been excruciating. Callan had stopped the man's interest, and the two had sent him away.

Her unease grew with anger. It was nighttime, and she hurt too much to sit. Turning over in the bed to cuddle Robbie, she saw a man sitting in her bedside chair. Aiden sat sleeping, hair mussed from running his hands through his hair. His beard was coming in, his stubble was as black as the hair on his head. She closed her eyes to fake being asleep.

"All right, Kayleigh. Hide now in the night. I will see you in the morning."

She kept her eyes closed.

****

Kayleigh awakened from her nightmare.

Oh my goodness. It was Aiden all along. He wears my ring. He lied for years. How was he able to do this? Maybe this was just a dream. No, I am awake. And I remember. His blue eyes looking into mine. Holding father's hand. Father giving me to Aiden who held my hand. I hope I don't have to play with him all the time. Brighde, Callan. They are my playmates. Must we allow Aiden to play? He's older. MacDonald tartan wrapped around our hands. We had to eat dinner tied together. Then he asked to speak to me alone. What would he do? Does he know how to play? What if he is boring? A boring old boy.

Kayleigh was devastated. How could he do this? How could he lie and not tell her they were handfasted? He tempted her into kisses and affection, which would have been permitted. Instead, she had guilt attached to all of it, even to him.

"Aiden!" She called at the top of her voice.

He came running upstairs. "Are you okay?" He burst into her room.

"You…you're a liar! How could you? You kept this secret from me. I wish I never remembered! You were nine years old. They never would have forced you to keep the secret. They would have considered my feelings. My emptiness, my hopelessness. The feeling no one could love me. The feeling I am not worthy of love. Did you ever stop to think of me? No. You didn't. Instead, you focused on yourself, your lack of a mate, your desires."

"I'm guessing you regained your memory. It isn't all

about you, you know. Even as a nine-year-old, when I made the promise, I meant it. Do you think it was easy on me? When I promised to love you always, I already did love you. It was the seed that would grow into a man's love. I never hid it from you. Even now, I have told you how I feel, facing rejection at every turn. Do you think it doesn't chisel at a man's pride? I asked what you value in me because I didn't know if there was anything you valued. It turned out you value me for what I had been forced to abandon. My honesty, my integrity. I hope we can overcome this. If any two were meant to be a couple, it is us. I believe we belong together."

"I don't know what to say. I don't think we can overcome this. I don't know what to believe. I don't want you. I don't even like you. Just leave me alone."

"It's all I need to know. Goodbye." And he left.

Chapter 13

Kayleigh discussed her memory recovery with Graeme in his office off the main hall.

"Graeme, he lied to me my entire life. I can't trust him. I can't bear the thought of him touching me. I want to be un-handfasted," she said.

"At least give him a chance as your husband, now you know," Graeme suggested.

"He is not an honest man."

"He's the most honest and dependable man I know."

"He lacks integrity. He has made a fool of me."

"Your pride's speaking. You don't know the real man, his most inner thoughts."

"I know all I need to know."

"I can't do this lightly."

"It is my sincere need to be parted from him."

"You need to think more on this."

She turned to look at him. "How long must I wait?"

"At least until Aiden returns. He must also agree to break the handfast bond and hold a parting ceremony."

"Of course, he will agree. He left, didn't he?"

"He was hurting. All of us saw it. He loves you, and you rejected him. You have rejected him before but never as your husband."

"I cannot call him husband. It is not what I want. I see no future for us."

"It will be uncomfortable for you to see him, to

patrol with him."

"It will be the same, except for no serene tree."

"Okay. We shall wait for his return."

Worried he might not agree, she returned to her room and sank into the bed, covered with a warm plaid. She was so cold Robbie curled up with her, purring.

****

He turned away from her, went downstairs, grabbed his always-packed knapsack, and left. *How can she believe I lied? Sure, I didn't tell her.* His anger lasted all the way past the apples and pears and past the third cave to his private cave. Callan would know where he had gone.

He sat in his cave with a bruised heart. An old oak tree blocked the cave. The first thing he had to do was build a fire for warmth and protection.

He lay a small pile of dried vegetation and tiny oak sticks which would easily catch fire. He set a larger pile aside to feed the fire later before it could catch the dead branches he had gathered. He also found larger logs to help the fire last through the night. One even had a rough bark on it, which made it last longer in the fire. He struck the flint to have an easy spark. He blew at the bottom of the pile for air circulation. It was important to amass enough kindling because the fire would die out before it caught on the larger branches unless there was enough kindling to keep feeding the small fire.

Then he loosely piled the tiniest of sticks on the flames. Larger sticks were placed to rest above the flames and draw the fire upward. He fed more dried matter into the then-empty space below the sticks. He kept the larger parts of branches near the fire to dry them out even more. He added progressively larger pieces, larger sticks, small branches, and larger parts of branches until the small logs caught fire. He waited patiently for each layer to catch. After they were burning, he added a few larger logs. He saved the very large ones for when the fire was secure so they wouldn't smother the fire when added. He also had a stack of logs from the last time he had gone camping. If he found more fallen branches or trees, he would use the axe stored in the cave to cut them to size. He needed the hard labor to work off his anger.

It wasn't long before he had a fire large enough to keep him warm. He had three stones, uniformly shaped ovals, stored in the cave. He added them to the fire. When they were white hot, he would remove one from the fire and let it cool enough to keep him warm through the night. He unrolled his bedroll near the fire.

He pictured Kayleigh there with him. For her, he would have built a larger fire, one like the hearth fire in the cave at Coire Gabhail. It had been the best fire, and she had built it herself. She was quite self-sufficient. Except she really wasn't. Everyone needed others if only to reflect who they were.

Who had he become? A man who storms out of the manor because he didn't get his way? He had always been there for her, without exception, until then. But he hurt deep inside. He had been confident of their love. Then she denied it. Not like her usual denial but in a wholly sincere way. She wouldn't let him touch her, had told him to go away. Now, here he was, away from her. He had pictured their future, now it was gone. He had been there for her her entire life. But others had not. She had been abandoned by her mother's death, her father leaving, and then by the man who had not loved her. It's a lot. Now here he was, abandoning her again.

He also had been abandoned by two parents' deaths and now by her, the single constant in his life besides his brothers. Who was he? An abandoned boy? The little boy in him still grieved Iain's death. It was the worst act of his life, not being able to rescue him. He flexed his muscles to remind himself he was now a strong man, the strongest of men. Yet he had been felled by a slip of a girl. Who was he kidding? She was no slip of a girl. She had grown into a strong woman, only a head shorter than him. Her head came to his chin. Her muscles had been developed by her archery and her running. She ran every day. She didn't lag behind him either. She kept up with his lighter form of running.

Man, there's a big hole inside me. Hopeless, devastated. Has love finally left me alone? He had wanted to grab her, shake sense into her. He had never felt it before, not with her. It had scared him and sent him away. He was disappointed in himself. He had never felt violence toward a woman. Not even Fiona had frustrated him so, as annoying as she was. If Kayleigh had not felt anything for him, he wouldn't have been so angered. But she loved him. One mistake had killed her love? One huge lifelong mistake. But he had been sworn to secrecy. What boy could keep a secret for so long? Had they expected a nine-year-old to make the vow? Probably not. But he had been a serious boy who wanted to maintain his integrity, to be honorable. It hadn't been even a year since Iain had died when they held the handfast.

When years later, he had asked Ilsa if he could tell Kayleigh, she had reminded him of the vow. Of her vow. So, maybe she couldn't give permission. But he hadn't been bound by the adults' vow. Like most children, though, he had followed the example set by the adults. It had made sense to him, even as a child. Let Kayleigh fall in love with him and not feel as if he had been forced on her. It would be her choice. But this very thing had broken her trust in him. If he had told her himself, had confessed to being her one true love…but it would have been ludicrous. *Good morning, Kayleigh. I am your one true love. Dearest Kayleigh, I am your true love. By the river, holding hands. Kayleigh dear, you may not know this, but I am your one true love. She would have laughed, been angry still, or thought me in the grasp of a fever.*

He became aware of a squirrel sitting near him and spoke to it. "I guess I have taken your home. I suppose I can share if you can. What am I saying? You don't live in the cave," *I am talking to a squirrel, nonsense. Squirrels don't live in caves.* "Though you may seek its shelter in the rain. But it's not raining now." It chattered at him, bringing two more squirrels to the cave entrance from the tree, one obviously younger than the other two. "Did I take part of your tree? If I did, it was only because it was lying dead on the ground." *No, you wouldn't be chattering and shaking your tail at me.* "What would Kayleigh do? She would feed you. You'd think I would have come to this conclusion a bit faster. Don't worry, friend. I have enough to share. But you, being a squirrel, already knew it. You must know Kayleigh. She's the one who feeds your relatives. Her image is in your guidebook to the forest eating places. You must be coming to me because I have often been seen in her company." He opened his food satchel, withdrew bread and cheese, and broke them into tiny pieces, catching them in his kilt. He stood and walked to the oak tree and put the food at the base of its trunk. The squirrels ran to it before he could move out of the way. His hunch had been correct. Two more squirrel families came to eat. He laid out more food and watched them until he became chilled, then sat by the fire, still watching the squirrels. *They are amazing creatures. They used their language to communicate with me, all the time knowing I had food to share. And the guide to the forest exists in their memory just like my internal guide to the forest exists in my memory.* At dusk, with the food gone, the squirrels returned to their trees. *Kayleigh's going to love hearing about this.*

Aiden awakened to light filtering into the cave, the soft light of dawn dissolving shadows. He stopped to blow the fire back to life before leaving the cave to relieve himself.

Sitting by the fire, he watched a wet patch dry on the cave wall. The smell of sulfur touched his nose. The sound of birds filled the air outside, and a breeze rustled the oak's leaves.

Alone again. Cave living is okay for a few days, but it has been a week. I miss home. Why am I here, still living in a cave? My anger is gone. What should I do now? Another week in a cave? No. I am used to my bed. She doesn't want to see me. I want to see her, though. I will always love her. She doesn't want me, doesn't even like me anymore. Even so, be a man and return home. She's not the only person there. I have family, and I need them now. I need to act, not react. I can still be dependable, loving. I may be hurting, but I don't need to act like I'm hurting. Callan would say, be a man. It's time to go home.

****

The next day, Aiden killed the fire and left food

remains for the squirrels and birds.

He reached the manor at dusk, hopeful Kayleigh would have changed her mind. He entered the manor. When she came downstairs, he lit inside. She didn't seem to see him at first. When she noticed him, she stopped short. Standing in place, she then turned around and ran back across the room and upstairs. She probably didn't stop running until she reached her room. She didn't look back as she ran. Was she afraid of him? No matter. He needed a bath anyway. Maybe it's what scared her. After a week in a cave, she probably smelled him and ran.

The water is warm. It will feel good to be clean again and to shave this itchy beard. A week without my bed. The comfort of a bed. I have missed the light in her eyes. I have become a sentimental sap. Back to the chase. What antics will she force me through this time? Back to patrolling, walking along, alert, but sharing our thoughts. Her laughter would be welcome. It took a week to regain hope. To think I was so fragile...

After the bath and the shave, he felt refreshed but bone weary. He fell into bed and covered up with his quilt. He thought of Kayleigh. Heart-warmed, he fell asleep.

He awakened the next morning to a knock on his door. Recognizing the knock, he opened the door to see Graeme standing there. He looked troubled, ran his hand through his beard, scratching his chin. "We need to talk, Aiden. Get dressed."

"I'll be there in a few minutes."

Graeme nodded, gave his beard one last tug, and left.

I wonder what trouble makes him need to speak to me now. He always waits until I go downstairs.

He dressed and went to speak with Graeme.

Graeme sat at the table, breaking his fast. Instead of the usual oats, he ate eggs, bacon, and thick slices of toasted bread with butter and jam pots on the table. Aiden's mouth watered at the sight and smell of his favorite meal. "Thank you, brother," he said, realizing Graeme had ordered it for his homecoming. Rose brought in his plate, and he relished every bite.

Graeme allowed Aiden time to finish his meal.

"We need to have a serious discussion," Graeme said, giving Aiden time to brace himself.

"What's wrong?" Aiden asked.

"Kayleigh is wrong."

"About what?"

"About you."

"Oh no." Still seated, he leaned on his elbows, head on his hands. He lifted his head and shook it, then leaned on his arms.

"What did she say?"

"She wants to undo the handfast. To hold a parting ceremony."

Aiden's heart plummeted. His chest ached, and his head hurt. Then he remembered his renewed, hopeful outlook. "I'll talk to her about it."

"She doesn't want to talk. She wants action."

"She doesn't know what she wants."

"She wants no husband. She is very clear about it."

"I'll convince her."

"You will not change her mind. Something seems to have died in her."

"I need to see her."

"She's already had her meal and went outdoors. Said she was going to the river."

"No!" Aiden ran outside and ran to the river. *Something died in her? I hope she won't do anything risky. There she is!*

Kayleigh was sitting on the bench by the river.

"Be careful!" he warned, moving between her and the river.

She stood and looked into his eyes. His worry was written on his face. "Aiden."

"We need to speak about this." He ran his fingers through his hair. "What happened?"

"What happened? You left me," she said. The light in her eyes had died. It was as if she had left. She stepped away from him.

"I left for a week. I'm back."

"It's too late. I don't want you." Her voice was monotone, steady.

He touched her ice-cold hand.

She stepped back, out of reach. Her eyes confirmed her words.

He touched her hands again. She moved away from him. And slipped back toward the river.

He caught her hands and pulled her to him, holding her close. "Be careful."

"Don't touch me. I don't want you near me," she said. Her expression never changed. She was serious.

He let her push him away from her. "I was just saving you from the river. If you don't want me touching you, I won't. Just step away from the river." He moved backward to give her room to move and to feel safe. "I love you but will not force you to be near me. I would give you anything."

"Even a parting ceremony?"

"Yes."

"Graeme said he would do it if you agree."

"I'll agree. I'll tell Graeme. We both need to be present."

"Thank you." She looked relieved.

Chapter 14

Aiden and Kayleigh returned to the manor. Heartsick, he walked a distance behind her.

They entered together.

Graeme waited for them in the Hall.

"Do it," he said to Graeme.

Brighde gasped. "Kayleigh, are you sure?"

A glimmer of hope lit Kayleigh's eyes.

"See her?" Aiden said. "It's what tells me this is the right thing to do. Give her what she wants. Make her happy again."

"Do you want it, Aiden?" Graeme asked.

"If she wants a Parting, then I want it. I want what's best for her."

"Okay. Now is as good a time as any."

Kayleigh twitched her lips as if to smile.

They faced Graeme together, though a step apart.

"Kayleigh, give me your ring," Graeme said, reaching out to her.

She removed it and snatched it back when he would have taken it.

"If you want this, then give me your ring and the chain," he said.

She gave them to him.

"Aiden, the same as Kayleigh."

Aiden removed the chain, kissed the ring, and gave them to Graeme, who placed both in a box from the mantle. Mairi lit the candle and dropped wax on the box to seal it closed. Graeme stamped it with his ring and returned the box to the mantle.

"You are no longer handfasted!" Graeme announced.

"Aren't you going to do anything more?" Kayleigh queried.

"What do you want me to do? I have never done this ceremony before."

"Untie us."

Graeme sighed. "Yes, okay. Callan, get my MacDonald ceremonial sword. Mairi, a strip of tartan, please."

Callan removed the ornate double-edged short sword from the wall where it was mounted and handed it to Graeme. Mairi returned, having removed a length of tartan from her workbasket.

"Brighde, tie the tartan around their hands and wrists. Use three knots, tying them so I can cut between them. Now, Kayleigh and Aiden, tell me what you want."

"I want to be Parted from Aiden MacDonald," Kayleigh said, her voice firm and steady.

"I want to be Parted from Kayleigh MacDonald," Aiden said, his voice cracked.

"Callan, stand behind Kayleigh," Graeme directed.

Callan moved behind Kayleigh, and Brighde moved behind Aiden. Mairi stood aside.

Graeme lifted the sword above their heads and sliced down to the center knot and had to use more muscle to cut through the knot.

Aiden fell to his knees, hands on the floor.

Kayleigh fell back into Callan's waiting arms.

"Kayleigh." Aiden groaned. His shattered heart lay at his feet. He tried to rise but couldn't.

"Mairi, give me the tartan," Graeme ordered.

As Graeme untied the other two knots, Kayleigh groaned and fainted. Callan carried her to her room. Mairi followed them.

Aiden fell from his knees to the floor. When Graeme threw the bonds into the fire, Aiden bellowed. He felt the fire. The sweat combined with the fire made it feel as if his skin was aflame. He passed out.

Aiden awakened on the floor hours later, still where he had fallen. He felt hollow and was aching all over as if he had influenza. His body was shaking beneath the plaid covering him.

"Make him sit," Graeme said, stroking his beard. "Make sure he drinks a lot."

Callan did so, and Mairi held a flask to his lips. He drank and drank more.

"Did you know this would happen?" Callan asked, his hands remaining on Aiden's shoulders as he stood behind him to keep him sitting up while he drank.

"Something was bound to happen," said Graeme. "Though nothing this extreme has happened before. I read about it in the family records when Kayleigh first mentioned the parting. It takes the Clan Chief to say the words. That makes it final," Graeme explained. "I read of one time the sword was necessary. The couple had been married fifty years and parted ways. They each needed a home after the parting and were given separate cabins."

"How awful. All those years together wasted." Callan sounded as if he mourned the parting.

"He has his color back," Mairi said, standing in front

of Aiden with hands on her hips.

"Not quite red anymore," Graeme said. "Still flushed, though." Relief sounded in his voice.

"I feel cold to the bone," Aiden said, pulling his tartan up around his shoulders.

"From lying on the cold floor," Graeme stated, rubbing his beard.

"Or the cold rug," Callan said. "For hours."

"How is Kayleigh?" Aiden wondered aloud.

"She's battling her demons," Callan said.

"After your fiery skin, Aiden, you needed the cold," Graeme stated. "Let's get you to your bed. Can you stand?"

"I'm weak," he said after trying to stand.

Callan and Graeme helped him stand, but he was wobbling, and they let him sit at the table. Rose brought out bread and cheese with meat from the previous night's meal and a pitcher of ale. She had cut the meat into small pieces.

"Aiden!" Kayleigh's yell reached them, and Aiden tried to stand.

"She's been calling for you," Callan said. "You need to strengthen yourself before seeing her. Brighde and Ilsa are with her."

"I feel so apart from her, so distant. I love her, but she is even farther away from me now."

"You two have a fresh start. Maybe you can fall in love," Callan speculated.

"Bite your tongue, man," Graeme exclaimed. "There are no records of reversal."

"Of course there aren't. They would have been recorded as handfasts," Callan answered.

"I'll hope for the best. Maybe she'll be happy

again," Aiden said.

"Aiden!" Kayleigh yelled.

He cringed, feeling the awareness skittle along his spine. He turned it off. He still loved her and wouldn't change it for anything.

"She'll hate me the rest of her life," Aiden spoke, disheartened.

"I still think the two of you will get back together," Callan declared. "She loved you and didn't want to admit it, even to herself."

"Will she have a separate residence?" Aiden enquired.

"No," Graeme said. "You will have to face each other at meals and throughout the day. How will you handle guard duty?"

"The same as always, except for the serene tree. She let me kiss her there."

"You'll need to ignore any leftover feelings," Graeme said.

"I will silence all residual feelings and not speak of them," Aiden said.

"You should, given time, express yourself," Callan said.

"On second thought, feel free to express yourself anytime," Graeme said. "Just be yourself."

"I will just be myself. I am going to see her now," Aiden turned to leave.

Callan began to speak.

"No, Callan. I need no more suggestions," Aiden said. "My mind is set."

Aiden left and went upstairs, hearing her call him one more time. He could hear her sobbing. His heart ached for her. He wouldn't wish her pain. They hadn't known the effect of the parting ceremony. Had he known the pain it would cause her, he would not have agreed to it.

He had thought it would make her happy. Maybe to be happy, she needed to cry.

****

"Aiden!" Kayleigh awakened to hear her own voice calling him. She felt so cold and empty.

"Kayleigh, dear. Are you awake?" Brighde asked.

"Yes. Where is he? He should be here," Kayleigh said. "Where is Aiden? Even the sound of his name hurts. Was I beaten again?"

"No."

"My throat hurts, and my eyes are sore."

"You have been crying."

"Is Aiden okay? What happened?"

"You got what you wanted most."

"Aiden."

"No, you requested a parting."

It all slammed back into her. The splitting headache, the ripping out of her heart. Where he had filled every fiber of her being was now empty. He had been taken away from her. The tears, so many tears. Her heart hurt as if he had died. "Is he dead? Please tell me if he died."

"He lives, but your bond was broken," Brighde responded.

"What bond? I was handfasted at four years old."

"But he was with you even when he wasn't present. He colored your thoughts. He was part of you. And you were part of him. I could see it. Everyone could see it. He cared more for you than for himself. It's why he agreed to break the handfast. He thought it would make you happy," Brighde said.

"I thought I would be happy too. Is he happy?"

"He fared worse than you did. Callan said Aiden felt the fire when the bonds were burned. He turned red and fainted with profuse sweating," Ilsa said. "He was unconscious for two hours. Though there's no blistering, he felt fire. He is eating now. Do you think you can eat?"

"Maybe broth to eat and a bit of whiskey."

"Here, can you sit?"

She sat up and drank the whisky. It was smooth, though it took away her breath.

"There, better, it brought back your color," Ilsa said.

"You're lucky you were unconscious when Graeme burned the tartan," Brighde said, eyes opened wide and eyebrows raised.

"I dreamed of fire. I dreamed of it burning Aiden. It hurt him, so he fell to the ground. I thought he was dead. I felt him no longer. You're right. He was part of me. It's part of me that is gone."

"We're hoping you and Aiden can rebuild those bonds, fall in love," Brighde said.

"It is exactly what I don't want."

"Graeme said you must stay unbonded for a month before you could handfast to him again," said Brighde.

"I said I don't want it."

"You need to know it is an option," Ilsa assured her.

"Of course, he won't want it either."

"You're in his soul, and he's in yours. Your souls remain attached. They were not burned. Don't be surprised to find your attraction, your souls' attraction, still exists," Ilsa said.

A tap on the door preceded Aiden's face appearing around the open door.

Ilsa welcomed him into the room.

"Aiden," Kayleigh breathed, regret filling her heart.

"You were calling for me."

"You were on fire in my dream. You called me to help you…in my dream. But I couldn't reach you. Then I awakened."

"You fainted. Callan carried you to your room," Ilsa added.

"I did feel the burning flames of fire," Aiden said. "If I had known it would cause you pain, I wouldn't have agreed to it."

"It felt as if you were ripped from my mind," Kayleigh said.

"I feel the same, except I still love you," he said.

"You need to wait a month before you can handfast again. I asked Graeme," Ilsa declared.

"Ilsa! Do not speak of it," Kayleigh ordered.

"Both of you need to know the options," she said.

"Thank you for telling me," Aiden said. "I intend to court you, Kayleigh."

"I won't have it." Kayleigh pouted, arms crossed. "Don't even think about it."

"Now you are a free woman. Don't you want attention from an old friend?"

"Friends, yes. We can be friends."

"And we will spend a lot of time together."

"Since we patrol together, it is true." Kayleigh felt she had lost control of the conversation and frowned. "Where will we take our breaks?"

"Don't worry. It won't be under the serene tree. Where would you like to go?"

"To the river. We could sit on a bench farther away from the river than before."

"I can do it. Just remain watchful of where you

stand. I respect the power of the river. You also need to respect it."

"I will respect it. River lunches. It could be fun with all the birds and the otters." She smiled.

"It's good to see you smile and to see you pout. You're already healing."

"I'll ignore what you say about pouting."

"Of course you will."

Kayleigh put her hand on her stomach as it growled. She swung her legs over the side of the bed.

"I'll take my leave now," he said. "See you at the table."

"If you decide to go away to the cave again, please tell us," Kayleigh said with an ascerbic voice.

"And tell us when you plan to return," Ilsa said. "All of us worried while you were gone."

"I will, though I don't expect to go," said Aiden. And he left.

With her stomach growling, they helped her put on her trews, boots, and a peach-colored tunic and went downstairs.

Aiden was sitting at the table, looking flushed, like he had a fever. She hadn't noticed when he came to see her. His cheeks and nose were red, and his arms were red. He had returned from his absence looking healthy and fit. He had given her what she wanted. What she had wanted was bad for both of them. He was eating broth and tiny bits of meat and a small helping of bread and cheese. A jug of ale was near his plate.

"Don't worry, dear, you'll have the same meal as Aiden. Pieces of meat small enough to digest. Sit and drink."

Her eyes met Aiden's. "How are you feeling? I

heard it was bad."

"I could handle it," he said.

"Of course you could handle it. Doesn't mean it wasn't bad."

"It was bad. Satisfied?"

"No. I'm sorry."

"Me too. Sorry."

"I know you blame me for your pain."

"I agreed to the plan. If there's blame to go around, it's mine."

"I'd say you have equal parts to blame for your circumstances," Callan noted.

"Callan, stay out of it," Brighde said.

"No one else is speaking here besides them," he said.

"Why not talk about whisky production or some such thing?" she said.

"Nothing new there," Graeme said.

"I was concerned for you," Kayleigh said, worry entering her voice.

"And I for you," Aiden responded as he lifted a fork full of eggs to his mouth.

She sneaked bits of cheese from her plate and upstairs into her room to feed them to Robbie, one at a time. He had to nose one hand or the other, telling which hand had the cheese in it. Of course, he knew where the morsel was hidden. Still, though, she said, "Good boy!" each time. Kayleigh repeated this until the cheese was gone, though she showed him the final piece before giving it to him. She raised two hands to show him the cheese was "all gone." He settled on one corner of the bed and gave himself a contented bath. It was then time for a catnap. Kayleigh closed her eyes, contented, mirroring her wee cat.

****

When she awakened, she considered the events of the day.

Aiden had been burning, red, and sweating like he had a fever. *I feel feverish myself, but then my nightmares of him burning weren't real nightmares.*

Am I so connected to him I felt his feelings? Have there been other times in my life when I have felt his pain? Yes, when his parents died. They were all in Caledonia while I was in Glencoe. Yet, my heart was pierced with his pain. Is this what I felt? The love. Was it his love for me or my love for him I was feeling? Probably both. I killed it, though. The parting, may I never hear it again, killed part of me. No, it was already gone when I awakened after the kidnapping. He didn't even stay to see how I was. I could have died. He was gone the next day.

He's not fully present. If he was, I would feel him. The bonds are gone. If I thought it would hurt so much, I wouldn't have asked for it. What have I become? How could I wish this on anyone, much less Aiden whom I loved. It's why it hurts so much, the big lie. He had all along been my one true love. No more. Who would have thought it could hurt so much? I had just remembered the handfasting when the fact he lied came crashing on me. He had been my trusted friend, my best friend. Then he was my love. Then my own true love. Can love be destroyed? It happened all at the same time, the warm handfast love, then the parting.

Does love exist? I love Brighde and Auntie. Maybe romantic love doesn't exist. Maybe it's all physical. After telling me he loved me over and over again, Aiden was gone. How could he do this to me, someone he was supposed to love so much? If love didn't exist, it would make sense. He never loved me at all. It's as though I don't exist, or a part of me doesn't exist. The romantic love is gone. Being loved is gone. The part of me who responded to his love is gone. Love is gone. Where did it go?

He said I could have what I wanted. I didn't want this. Can we change back to how we used to be? In love with each other? No. Not after what has happened. It's the end of love. But Auntie said we could begin again. She talked about soul love. Maybe there's a wee bit of love left. If we had soul love like she thinks, then all the love can't be gone. I need to live as if love is alive, not dead. Like we could find love again. Am I able to feel love again? Yes. Auntie's soul love. I am a strong woman. I can love again.

There was a knock on her door.

"Kayleigh, you have visitors." Ilsa was at the door.

"Can they come back later?"

"There's a special little visitor who wants to be sure you're okay now after being kidnapped."

"Oh, a special visitor?"

"Little Gabe and Fiona are downstairs."

"I'll be right there."

"Are you sure?"

"Yes."

She dressed and went downstairs.

"Miss Kayleigh!" Gabe said. He would have run to her, but Fiona had a firm grasp of his hand.

"Gabe. Fiona. Thank you for visiting. Come sit with us."

"Thank you, Kayleigh. We want to be sure you're

okay. We heard you had an episode today."

They sat with Brighde. Rose brought them juice and biscuits.

Gabe stared at Kayleigh. Then he stared at Fiona, who sat next to him. He looked back and forth.

"Miss Kayleigh, your bruise matches Miss Fiona's bruise. It's pretty. Light green. The color is just like a baby dragon," said Gabe.

"A baby dragon?" said Kayleigh.

"Dragons. He's been talking non-stop about dragons, dragon color, dragon behavior, dragon names."

"We are studying fantastical creatures in school this week," Brighde said, clarifying his words.

"Ah, I see. Dragons are fun creatures," Kayleigh said.

"They fly and they breathe fire," he said.

"He's been watching the sky and hoping to see one. They are imaginary Gabe," Fiona said.

"It's true," Kayleigh agreed. "But it's fun to think of them anyway, right?"

"As long as a child knows the difference between what's real and what's not real," Fiona said. "It's what Bryan says."

"Yes, though children need a good round of play every day. They can pretend things are real. Better they pretend now and not wait until adulthood," Brighde said. "Then they would become confused about what's real."

"You're right," Fiona said. "I need to discuss this with Bryan. He doesn't take criticism well."

"He can come talk with me about it," Brighde said.

"Ah yes. The voice of authority. It might be the way to go," Fiona agreed.

"The way to go," Gabe repeated.

"Oh dear," Brighde said. "Pretend is the way to go."

"Let's hope he remembers you said pretend," Fiona laughed.

"It will work out. I'm happy to see you, and Bryan, and Gabe together," Brighde said, a teasing lilt to her voice.

"Me too. It's nice to see," Kayleigh said.

"You look tired," Fiona said. "I hope you feel better soon."

"I will. It just takes time," Kayleigh said.

"We'll go home now. Say goodbye, Gabe," said Fiona.

"Bye, Miss Kayleigh, Miss Brighde. 'Night," said Gabe.

"Good night," said Kayleigh.

Gabe waved, looking over his shoulder, as he and Fiona went outdoors.

"It looks like Fiona is at home in Caledonia. What about you?" Brighde asked.

"Before the kidnapping, I would have said I was starting to feel at home here," Kayleigh answered.

"We all love you here," Brighde said.

"Thank you, sister."

Chapter 15

"I'm glad you met me here by the lavender," Aiden said. "It's peaceful and somewhat public. I thought you would be comfortable here."

"I'm not sure why I came," Kayleigh declared.

"Maybe you don't want to lose a friend."

"Maybe."

"We had a lifelong friendship built on trust. Do you understand why I couldn't tell you?"

"I think so. You took a vow of silence about the handfast. I was so shocked it was you, I reacted poorly. But then you left me. You left without giving me time to explain. And I had just been kidnapped."

"I am sorry. It wasn't the right thing to do. I should have been here for you. I'm glad your bruises are fading. I'm here now, giving you whatever it is you need from me."

"Ripping out those bonds was painful," Kayleigh said.

"I had a fever from it and now emptiness inside," Aiden agreed. "I'm still within you. Some of what we had remains in us. I can feel it."

"How can I feel it too?" Kayleigh said.

"Look inside yourself. You'll see I'm still there. I wasn't wiped out of you any more than you have been taken from me. Bonds may be gone, but deep, soul-shattering love remains. The bonds aren't all gone. They were attacked, but our love is deep enough to survive it. You're part of me. I'm part of you. This will never change," he said.

"Then why do I feel so empty, so apart from you?" she asked.

"I don't know. Maybe you don't feel what I feel. Maybe it's all an illusion. But I believe we need to try to be close again. Can we meet and talk every day, set a special time aside for talking? May I take you to the river or to the tree?"

"To the river, yes. The tree's too private and holds too many memories. Maybe in time. The lavender keeps me calm, though."

"I love you, Kayleigh."

"Thank you."

****

A week later, Aiden and Kayleigh sat together on a bench by the river. He held her hand in his. "Please consider marrying me, Kayleigh. I love you and have always loved you."

"We still have three weeks to think about this." She turned to face him.

"Consider my feelings," Aiden said. "My whole life, it has been you."

"I have always been wife of your heart," she said. "However, you have never been husband of my heart."

"But you were in love with me. I know this to be true."

"I can't. Right now, I can't do it."

"I'll not beg. You let me take liberties with you."

"I didn't!" She stood, hands on her hips.

"You let me hold your hand, kiss you."

"Those are courting behaviors," she corrected him.

"My point exactly."

"Let's discuss the birds. There are more birds in Caledonia," she said, reaching for another topic.

"Yes, a greater variety than Glencoe. Hawks, and other beautiful birds, the orioles, the osprey, and the cardinals."

"I love the squirrels best. They're so cute! The otters too. So playful. They make me laugh."

"Yes, they are cute," he said.

Their eyes met, and she laughed. "I am being silly."

"To the contrary, you are refreshing. You see Caledonia through new eyes and make me see it anew."

****

"I remember when you used to look at me, everything else would fade," Kaleigh said. "Only you would exist. Nothing else. When anyone interrupted, it would startle me like being shaken awake from a deep sleep. Now, though, it's like you're not here, not present. It's as if you're the one who has faded away. Except you were ripped away, not even close to fading. How can we even be friends if you aren't here?"

"I am here. I'm not a memory. I'm real," Aiden said. "I am still your friend, and we were even more than friends. We still are. Yes, we were ripped apart from each other. But we can rebuild what we had. I still love you. I love you, Kayleigh. I have always loved you. It will never stop. I hope you can love me again."

"I don't know if it's even possible. It often hurts just being near you. The emptiness is overwhelming."

"As long as we talk about it, we'll be okay. It will take time to get used to this."

"If we can ever get over it." Kaleigh worried it wouldn't work.

"At least when we're talking about us, there is an us."

They walked to the river, sat on the bench, and spread out a meal. Meat pies, both bigger than her hand. She picked the smaller of the two and looked into Aiden's eyes as she bit into it. He gave a toothy, lopsided smile as he bit into his pie, which was larger than his hand too. It reminded her of how tiny her strong hand felt in his when they'd held hands before. The last time was a month prior to today. They had made it two weeks as friends.

After they feasted on the food, he put three pieces of sewn, stuffed cloth on the bench between them.

"What's this?" Kayleigh said.

"Look at them, pick them up."

One was a bird, the second had the face and ears of a mouse, and the third looked like a big piece of cheese.

"Toys for Robbie. What a thoughtful gift." She tucked them in her pockets. "I'll roll them in cat herbs. Did Ilsa make them? Let's return to our patrol."

"I requested them for you. She has many skills."

Kayleigh let him assist her from the bench.

"He will be so happy."

"Aiden? I have a question."

"I hope I have an answer for you."

"It's about Dougal. What happened to him? Was he banished?"

"He is now staying as a *guest* with the Campbells for three years. His mother had been captured. She was set free and now lives in Caledonia. If he returns, he will be on house arrest for five years. If those eight years do not correct him, we will have no recourse but to send him to Fort William."

"I'm glad he's gone."

They walked back to the manor. She reached for his hand and held it. His blue eyes lit, crinkled with his smile. He swung their arms. She felt filled with happiness because she had made him happy, and she smiled back at him. They arrived at the manor to find Brighde planting seedlings.

"I want to help," Kayleigh said.

"You're welcome to help. Have you ever done this before?"

"No, but I'm not afraid to get dirty."

Eyeing her immaculate, clean shirt, Brighde said, "You might want to change to an old dress you have."

"Skirts? No thanks. I'll get an old shirt. Besides, I don't wear skirts enough for them to grow old."

Aiden went indoors with her.

When she returned, she sat on the ground cross-legged.

Brighde sat on a short stool facing her across the garden row.

"What are we planting?" Kayleigh asked.

"Bluebell seedlings. They've been hardened off," Brighde answered. She picked up another seedling and handed it delicately to Kayleigh.

"They're hard?"

"They have become hardy. If they don't, then they'll never make it through the seasons."

"Here's a planting trowel. Dig about so deep, like this."

Kayleigh followed her actions and dropped the seedling into the hole. She put aside the trowel and used her fingers to dig.

"No, like this." Brighde gently held the seedling so

the roots dangled into the hole. With gentle care, she dropped soil back into the hole. "Allow the soil to surround the roots. Like this." She tapped the top of the tiny mound of soil with her fingers.

"There's too much room there. How will the roots grow in the hole left there?"

"There's space at the very bottom. Lightly packed soil fills the hole. It will drop and balance without us forcing extra soil."

"What do the plants eat?"

"The roots will seek the soil nutrients. They will spread and grow into the soil," Brighde said. This is a mix of the old soil and the new soil. So, it isn't completely new to the seedlings. They're a bit used to it."

"Now I see why you come back from the solarium so dirty."

"I tend to wipe my hands on my skirts. You have yet to wipe yours."

"I have a rag in my pocket."

"You're smart, dear."

"I can tell you're a good teacher. You're patient and good at explaining," said Kayleigh.

"You should see the children trying to understand math. Some can't follow and may never be good at it. Others take to it right away. The girls tend to apply themselves to studying, though there are exceptions both ways, boys and girls. You are a good student. It comes from all your lessons with Aiden. He taught you all those defenses. You learned math when he tutored you."

"He was patient and would challenge me. He traded an hour of math for an hour of archery."

"Ah, he was smart about it."

147

"He's very intelligent, as you know."

"Don't you love him at all?"

"Yes, I suppose I do. It must be the soul love Ilsa mentioned."

"Soulmate."

"Mate? I don't think so." She shook her head.

"Why are you afraid of the word 'mate?'"

"Blake, the one who claimed he loved me and had me believing he was my own true love, decided he liked Fiona better because she—"

"I know what Fiona does. She goes from man to man, looking for love."

"Yes, it's why I don't like the word."

"But 'soulmate' is a beautiful thing. It's when two hearts and two souls are made for each other. One soul can't live without the other."

"Can there be more than one soulmate?"

"No. There is one. For instance, I have no doubt you and Aiden are soulmates. He loves you. I saw you holding hands and saw the expression in your eyes, soft and lit like candles were lighting your eyes."

"I need to think about this for a while."

"You have two more weeks to wait for a new—"

"Don't say it."

"Handfasting." It seemed Brighde couldn't resist.

"Now you've chased me away."

"We're finished anyway. You can't fool me, sister."

Kayleigh left to enter the manor. She decided she would hold Aiden's hand whenever they were together, except on patrol.

Chapter 16

Early in April, the family gathered for Kayleigh's birthday.

Here's my gift for you." Aiden handed her a basket. "The lavender-scented soap was my mother's. We have a lot of the soaps. She kept all the soaps she made for herself." He laughed. "The recipe was given from mothers to daughters. I made the lavender-scented candles with Ilsa's guidance. There's also a small bottle of lavender oil."

Kayleigh laughed with delight. "You even tucked in lavender-colored ribbon. Thank you so much. What a thoughtful gift."

"I remember you love Ilsa's lavender."

"My mother also made lavender-scented candles. You have given me part of my mother." She set the basket on the table and rose to kiss his cheek and hug him. "No one knows me the way you do." His cheeks flushed as he smiled.

She sat again to open Ilsa's gift, a lavender blouse with pearl buttons. She kissed Ilsa's cheek and thanked her.

Brighde gave her eight more candles. Mairi made her a lavender-colored satchel tied with a lavender ribbon. Callan gave her a set of lavender ribbons for Beauty, and Graeme gave her fresh lavender leaves to make scent packets for her clothes. Kayleigh kissed the women's cheeks, but not the men, except for Aiden.

Dinner was Kayleigh's favorite, Rose's stew. There was one large apple pie on each of the tables in celebration. The crisp smell of apples permeated the room.

"I have an idea," she said.

Everyone at the table stopped speaking to look at her.

"I want us to grow enough lavender so every cabin and cottage has a bunch of lavender. Everyone should have it."

"Unless the occupants sneeze at it," Callan said.

"Of course," she said.

"It's a good idea," Graeme added. "Brighde, do you think it can be done?"

"Yes, and Kayleigh will assist me."

"Kayleigh?" Ilsa wondered as she looked at her.

"I helped her plant the new bluebell garden," Kayleigh folded her arms in defense.

"We'll get the community lavender by thinning out the older gardens," Brighde said. "My favorite flower is the little white rose."

"Mine is the pink rose," Mairi said with a sigh.

"Years ago, before you girls were born, a gentleman caller brought me a large pink rose and called it an English Beauty," Ilsa said.

"What happened to him, Auntie?" Brighde asked.

"He was visiting Glencoe for a month. Then he left. I never heard from him again. I never met another."

"Was he your soulmate?" Kayleigh wondered. She realized everyone was listening to their conversation. "Oh, don't answer Auntie."

"There is one soulmate for each person. Their souls

want to be together." Ilsa said. "Now, let's focus on Kayleigh for her birthday."

Kayleigh exchanged a long look with Aiden. *Is he my soulmate, my own true love? I think he might be.* She smiled at him. *Oh no, everyone saw it.* And she blushed. Her family must have seen the blush because they smiled too.

"Thank you, everyone, for the gifts, the attention. Today is why birthdays should be celebrated. It made me feel special."

"You are special, dear," Brighde said.

"Come walk with me, Kayleigh," Aiden said.

He placed her cloak on her shoulders, then put on his own.

He held the door open for her, and they went outside.

They held hands as they walked to the bluebell path.

"What were you thinking about when our eyes met?" he said.

"I was wondering if maybe we are soulmates," she said.

"Thanks for your honesty. And if we are soulmates?"

"Then there is no one else for either of us."

"Neither of us is looking for someone else," said Aiden. "Are you?"

"Am I what?" said Kayleigh.

"Looking for someone else."

"No."

"Neither am I."

She opened and closed her mouth.

"What were you going to say?"

"I was going to say you shouldn't be looking for

someone else."

"Neither should you."

"What if we made a terrible mistake?" said Kayleigh.

"I think we did make a mistake. I love you even more than I did before."

"I need to think about this."

"We have a week until we can handfast."

"Let's not rush this."

"I feel certain now but will cultivate patience."

"I'm afraid to feel certain."

She stopped walking and faced him. She reached and cupped his face and placed the lightest of kisses on his lips. Then she groaned and kissed him harder. He gathered her to him and kissed her with passion. He cradled her face and ended with a whisper of a kiss.

They joined hands and walked back indoors.

"Are you ready—" said Callan, until Brighde hit his arm.

"What a beautiful day," said Kayleigh. "I'm going to gather my presents and retire for a while."

"Let me help you," said Brighde.

"Me too," said Mairi as she rose to accompany them.

****

Kayleigh sat on her bed, Brighde and Mairi with her.

"You have not needed a nap since you were a child. Those forced on you by Ilsa when younger don't count," Brighde accused.

"I still need naps," Mairi said.

"It's because of your injury and…" Brighde added.

"Kayleigh was injured in the kidnapping and doesn't take naps," Mairi said.

"Brighde is right," Kayleigh agreed.

"It depends on how you feel," Mairi said.

"What did you and Aiden discuss?" Brighde asked with curiosity.

"The flowers, my presents…" Kayleigh said.

"You lie," Brighde accused, shaking her finger at Kayleigh.

"Do tell," Mairi encouraged. She leaned forward, eyebrows raised.

"We held hands. And talked about soulmates," Kayleigh said with a sigh.

"Does he think you are his soulmate?" Mairi wondered.

"Yes," Brighde declared.

"Yes, he does. But here's the thing, I think he might be my soulmate. This would mean we did a terrible thing," Kayleigh admitted. "I miss the bond we had. I mean he's still there and we're forming new bonds. But the feeling of him always being present is gone."

"Do you think you will do it again?" said Mairi.

"Handfast? I think it is an option," Kayleigh said. "It would be my first voluntary one, where I make a promise."

"At least she can say the word now," Brighde said.

"And it's an option," Mairi confirmed.

"Does Aiden know?" Brighde asked.

"Yes, I told him," Kayleigh said.

"What did he say?" Mairi asked.

"He said he would be patient," Kayleigh said.

"I would have swooned," Brighde said, hand on her forehead, as she fell back on the bed.

****

Hidden by a large weeping willow tree, Aiden and Kayleigh stood close, facing each other.

"You know I still love you. In fact, I love you more than ever." Aiden hoped she would return his feelings. They had grown together over the past weeks.

"I care more for you than ever before," she said. "I think I love you, though I don't really know what love is. Is it when my heart longs for you? When making you happy makes me happy? When we hold hands and other parts of me feel warm and tingle?"

"Yes, love is all of it, plus physical attraction," Aiden said. "Do you feel it?"

"I think I do. I want you to kiss me and to touch me," Kayleigh said.

He touched her shoulders and bent to kiss her. She put her arms around his neck and pulled him closer. He hugged her and stepped back.

He cupped her face with his hands, and his lips caressed hers. He deepened the kiss and held her closer. She felt his passion increase and liquid fire traveled up her spine.

"Oh, my…" She fell against him for a moment. "What happened?"

"Physical passion," he said and rubbed against her again.

"It feels so good," Kayleigh whispered.

"Yes, it does, but we need to stop here today," he said, and stepped back from her. They held hands as they walked out from the privacy of the weeping willow.

Chapter 17

"I will wear boots beneath the gown," Kayleigh said, filled with ire. "Everyone at the dance will see them.

"Don't you want Aiden to see your ankles?" Brighde asked.

"I don't want to tempt him more than I already do."

"He has said so?"

"He asked me to marry him."

"A proposal?"

"Not exactly. It was a question, a suggestion."

"What did you say? No, let me guess. You're not ready."

"Yes. I suppose you plan to tantalize Callan with glimpses of your ankles."

"Yes, I do. Your sentence was worthy of Aiden himself. Auntie will not be pleased about the boots."

"Aiden uses too many big words."

"And had the same tutor we had."

"Auntie will not see the boots. I do not plan to dance, and my skirts will dust the ground."

"Right. I would like to see you deny Aiden at his most charming."

"You're right. It would be hard to do."

****

"You know she will wear boots with the gown," Aiden laughed upon being shown the blue swatch by

155

Ilsa.

"I ordered boots to match," she said. She pulled out a satchel and removed a pair of blue boots trimmed with tiny pearls.

"Those are fancy boots, too fancy for Kayleigh. She'll not like the pearls."

"She'll wear them if you give them to her."

"It's a great idea. And Brighde?"

"I'll give her new pink slippers. And I ordered green to match Mairi's dress."

"Kayleigh will see through our ruse."

"She will wear them. I'll be satisfied."

"You know your girl."

"She might as well be my daughter."

"Though they call you Auntie, you are their mother in all ways except birth."

"I wish my sister was alive to see the girls, to enjoy them."

"If she was alive, I would be a happily married man."

"Yes, when Ellen passed, so did Kayleigh's memory of the handfast. They happened too close in time."

"I asked her to marry me. She's not ready yet. Still, she is the woman for me. Do you think she would wear my mother's pearl necklace?"

"I don't think so."

"Suppose Mairi and Brighde also wear her jewelry?"

"It might work. Yes, it's a perfect idea."

****

Dressed in the blue ankle-length frock, blue boots, and pearl necklace with flowers in her hair, Kayleigh stood watching the people go by. The girls all seemed drawn to Aiden and Callan. Aiden was kind enough to speak with each one. *Callan is a peacock. Look at him, flirting with all the women. Introducing himself, bowing over their hands. You'd think the Spring Festival was a hunt for his mate when Brighde is the right choice. Brighde is of interest to the men, though they hang back following her, Graeme, and Mairi. Mairi's hand is tucked into Graeme's arm. The rest of us should be following their example. Aiden's muscles are on display in the kilt he wears. Now I'm hot. He is a fine specimen, as Callan would say about the women. His hair isn't tied back today, and his sparkling blue eyes are always watching me. His shoulders so strong, his wide, thick chest under his open shirt. His chest lightly covered with dark hair feathering down.*

His strong stomach, thighs, and calves. Some of the men's legs are spindles by comparison. Their chests appear bare or furry. Arms too thin or out of proportion with their bodies. I can see most of his body today. What beauty. Why is the word 'beauty' saved for women? He is beautiful. If I married him, I could see everything. Touch everything.

"Aiden is looking fine today, isn't he?" Fiona, who appeared to be salivating over him, asked. She smirked at Kayleigh. "He's a fine specimen, no?"

"Indeed he is, but we already knew it. It isn't news."

"Do I detect jealousy on your part? Shall we vie for his attention?"

"Not interested in a contest."

"Oh yes, you leave your competition for archery. Not for men."

"I scored!" Aiden flashed by and returned to twirl Kayleigh around and away from Fiona.

"Thank you."

"Nothing to thank me for. I want to be with you."

Damn, he smells good. Sweaty and good. Mmm.

They danced and twirled to the music of a fiddle, finishing with both of his hands on her ribs just below her bosom. She was smiling at him, and he kissed her. Heat filled her, and she swayed. He kissed her again, a light, sensuous kiss, moving his lips over hers, ending with a resounding smack.

She looked at his dancing eyes, filled with laughter and heat. He hadn't looked at her like this since…he hadn't ever looked at her like this…with such joy!

They watched Gabe win a second-place ribbon in the boys' archery group a year older than him. Kayleigh didn't compete. Instead, she rooted for Callan, who didn't win. *I will wear trews next year and compete. This is home now.*

"Look at Bryan and Fiona and Rose and Ian. They look happy," said Aiden.

Fiona and Bryan danced close together. Fiona rapt with attention on him.

****

After the festival, Kayleigh lay back on her bed.

He believes we were meant to be together. When he told me I would become the best archer in Caledonia, I loved being told. What a thing to say! I loved him then. He was so sincere. He taught me to use a dagger and to throw knives. And when he learned to swim, he taught me so I wouldn't drown like his brother. He picked me out of all the Glencoe and Caledonian girls. I must be special to him. I was special to him even then. There he was with a suspicious little girl. I was four. He was nine. He wanted me to be happy. It's all he wanted. He wanted to make me happy. It's what he wants now, to make me happy. How will I tell him I am ready?

Why did I forget? Mama died soon after the handfast. Auntie would say I wanted to forget about Mama passing, so other things then were also forgotten. I forgot how he doted on me in the spring. He brought me wildflowers, a crown of flowers, a piece of candy, and new arrows he carved for me. He made a new quiver every few years as I grew. There was the year I filled out, and he had to make an adjustable strap. He blushed as he put it on me. Oh, how I love him. Why can't I say it?

Chapter 18

Kayleigh walked in the lavender garden, thinking of Aiden. She had just turned toward the river when she heard a child scream. She ran to help the child bobbing in the river and waded in, but the current pulled her into the river. She tried to tread water and was pulled under again and again.

Aiden had planned to meet her at the bench and saw it. He disrobed and ran to where the child bobbed. He dove in and swam to reach the child who was farther away from Kayleigh. He grabbed the back of the child's shirt and lifted him to breathe. Head above the water for a moment, Aiden got a good breath. He swam near the shore and gave Gabe to Bryan. He then swam toward Kayleigh, who was gasping for air as she was pulled under. Her strength was gone as she stayed under longer each time she sank and then didn't surface at all.

By then, Aiden's breathing was rough. Solid as a stone, he sank and grabbed the leg of Kayleigh's trews as she tumbled by. He held her with one arm, head above the water, and swam to shore, where Callan and Brighde reached for Kayleigh. He saw Bryan with Gabe and gave thanks. *This time, I was strong enough to rescue the child.*

Ilsa brought Aiden a plaid.

Seeing Kayleigh lying on the ground inert, his labored breathing turned into sobs. He pulled the plaid around himself and stood there, eyes on Kayleigh. *She was mine, my own true love.*

"Aiden, you need to return to the manor," Graeme's voice was gentle.

"Can't."

"You'll catch your death of cold."

"It won't matter. If she's gone, nothing will matter."

He watched Callan and Brighde working over Kayleigh's inert body. After Iain died, the tutor had been charged with teaching how to revive drowning victims. He had found an old Greek text which described the method. Kayleigh had been placed lying face down, and head turned. Callan knelt at her head, her arms stretched toward him. He held her upper arms and rocked back. It took four times stretching her arms toward him for her to begin retching up the water. Brighde knelt at Kayleigh's side, moving the water away from her mouth. Callan continued until it looked like she was trying to breathe. The coughing stopped. One more stretch and she spewed the last of the water and shuddered with a deep breath.

She lives. Thank God. I almost lost her.

****

Kayleigh spluttered awake. Disoriented at first, she wondered why she was on the ground. Her chest and throat hurt. She saw Brighde looking at her very close. She and Callan turned her over, supporting her head with a rolled plaid.

"You drowned, dear," said Brighde.

It all came rushing back. *The boy in the water, running into the water. The shocking cold water. Gabe, carried away too fast for her to catch him. Being swept away by the rushing river. Her strength sapped by loss of air. Choking. Sinking down, down, sleepy, peace. I drowned. Who saved me?*

"Aiden rescued you and Gabe," Callan said, sitting by her.

"Let me help you sit, dear," Brighde said to Kayleigh as she placed a blanket around her.

Sitting, she looked over and found Aiden with tears dripping down his cheeks.

"Aiden. Thanks…my life," said Kayleigh. "Gabe?" She looked around.

"He's going to be fine. He's already asking for you," Brighde said.

"I told you, Aiden," Kayleigh said. "You are good…honorable…love you."

"I didn't save you. Callan and Brighde did. They worked over your body until you breathed. They remembered the drowning training," Aiden grasped the blanket Ilsa gave to him.

"You dove into the water and rescued her so Brighde and I could do it. You saved them," Callan said.

"Kayleigh lying there dead is a vision I'll never forget. I'm grateful she lives. Grateful for you and Brighde," Aiden said, shivering and shaking.

"Let's get everyone back indoors." Brighde stopped walking for a moment. When she started crying, Callan pulled her close.

Graeme lifted Kayleigh into his arms.

****

A day later, Aiden sat on a chair in Kayleigh's room and watched her sleep. Robbie lay beside her, squinting his eyes at him. He found himself blinking back at the cat.

"Aiden?"

It was but a whisper. He knelt on the floor beside her

bed and held her hand.

"Save your voice," he said.

"I love you...all this time...loved you."

"I know you did. Thank you for telling me, love."

"Sorry I made you wait."

"I love you. There is nothing I wouldn't do for you."

"Now we love together," she said. "Soulmates."

"Marry me?" he asked.

"Yes."

"Today?"

"Yes."

****

They arrived for breakfast together and were quiet throughout the meal.

"Someone break the silence, please," Callan said. "And pass the butter."

Graeme reached across Brighde and handed Callan the butter.

"Bread," Aiden said, handing it across the table to Callan.

Kayleigh shifted in her seat.

"You're restless today, Kayleigh. You look refreshed. Is there something you want to say?" Brighde's eyes searched hers.

Kayleigh looked at Aiden, who met her look.

"You are restless today." Aiden nodded his agreement.

She turned to face everyone, being near the head of the table next to Graeme. "I want to thank all of you. Thank you for saving my life."

"You're welcome."

"It's fine."

In turn, each of them expressed appreciation for her

thanking them.

"I had a breakthrough this morning," she said, her face and neck flushing.

"Tell us," Brighde urged her sister.

Kayleigh decided it was better to share the news with everyone present.

"I love Aiden and will marry him."

"Oh, sweet Kayleigh. It's wonderful," Brighde was obviously delighted.

"Tell us what you're thinking," Callan said.

"I think this conversation is best left for Aiden and Kayleigh," Graeme pushed his chair back to stand.

Mairi remarked, "It's about time you two were together. What I don't understand is why the handfast was a secret."

"Our parents wanted us to fall in love. I fell in love the instant the chain holding her ring was placed around my neck." Aiden pointed at Kayleigh, sitting in her place next to Graeme. "She looked into my eyes and questioned the choice."

"I questioned the choice they made for me. I didn't question it was you," Kayleigh said.

"You said, 'a husband should have yellow hair.' Aiden has black hair. Mine was yellow," Callan said with a smirk.

"I was a child and more familiar with you. I thought the handfast meant I would have to play with Aiden. He was nine years old. I was four. Though he did help me improve my aim with the bow."

"What about later when we all shared a tutor?"

"As I grew, I fancied Aiden, but he showed no interest. He was all business, giving me archery lessons, teaching me to use a dagger. I even had fancy fighting lessons. None of the boys would approach me for fear of Aiden."

"You make me out to be a monster," Aiden said. "I focused on teaching my future wife to defend herself. You made yourself a great archer all by yourself."

"As soon as Aiden and Callan returned to Caledonia each winter, the boys would seek us out," Brighde smiled.

"And Auntie made me wear skirts," Kayleigh complained.

"Is this true?" Aiden demanded of Ilsa.

"Yes, of course," she said. "Your word had no sway over me when you left in autumn."

"I wanted her to grow to be her own woman," he said.

"And am I not my own woman?" Kayleigh said.

"Whose side are you on?" Aiden asked.

"My own side."

"Our parents insisted we marry, but I chose Kayleigh," he said. "Come sit by me." He patted the seat next to him.

The others left the room.

****

Kayleigh went around the table to sit by him.

"I love you. I have always loved you. Even before the handfast. My father consulted with me prior to then. He told me I would be handfasted and asked who I would have. At nine years old, I knew it was you I would marry," Aiden brushed his fingers over her palm.

Her heart lifted. *He loves me. Just like I am.* "How could you know?"

"Even then, you made my heart sing. You still do."

"I don't know what to say. Except, I love you. I

mean, I have always loved you in a respectable way. Now I love you—"

"In a disrespectful way?"

"Stop, or I'll never say it all."

"Okay."

"I've been attracted to you ever since you put your sixteen-year-old arms around me to help sharpen my aim. I have loved you all along, I think. I didn't know you were my own true love, so I fought against it. Then, when I saw the ring you wore and knew you had your own true love, I had to turn from you, though it broke my heart. Then, when you left, it pierced my soul."

"I'm so sorry I didn't tell you."

"I love you in a romantic way. You are my own true love. I will love you forever."

He cupped her face and kissed her with utter tenderness.

****

"Are we ready for the rings now?" said Graeme as they returned to the room.

Mairi held the length of tartan needed.

"We have been tried by fire," Aiden announced.

"And by pain and loss," Kayleigh said.

"Brighde, tie their hands together," Graeme said.

"One knot is sufficient," Aiden ordered.

They held hands and were tied together.

"This ceremony undoes the previous one, restoring the bonds which were broken," Graeme said. "These two souls are a match unlike any other and become one."

Graeme retrieved the little box from the mantle. He removed the rings from the chains and gave the rings to the couple.

Aiden kissed her ring and placed it on her finger. "I

love you, now and forever, Kayleigh of Caledonia, mate of my soul.

Kayleigh kissed his ring and placed it on his finger. "I love you, now and forever, Aiden of Caledonia, mate of my soul."

They both knelt, eyes closed.

"It's too much…overwhelming," Aiden said. *I feel you inside me. Kayleigh, can you hear me?*

I can hear you, came her thoughts. *Oh, Aiden, I can feel you, hear you inside me. It's not hearing, but more.*

Graeme interrupted them by lifting them to their feet.

It's like you are in every fiber of my being, Aiden thought.

Yes, in every bit of me, Kayleigh thought.

"Why aren't you speaking?" Brighde asked.

"We can hear each other's thoughts," Kayleigh told her and everyone else in close proximity.

"You told them," Aiden teased her. "We could have kept it secret."

"But who's going to believe us, anyway?"

"I believe you," Graeme said. "The way you felt the loss tells me you shared one another's presence even before the parting."

"I believe you too," Ilsa said. "Yours is a rare love."

"I'll remain skeptical," Callan couldn't seem to keep his ascerbic wit to himself.

"We're soulmates," Kayleigh laughed with joy in her heart.

"Indeed," said Ilsa.

Hello soulmate. Aiden smiled.

Hello soulmate. Kayleigh smiled.

"They just did it!" Brighde said.

"You're right. We did," Kayleigh said.

"Let's have our celebration. Whether it be survival from the river or rejoicing in the handfast, today we have a celebration of life," Graeme pronounced.

Everyone sighed, exclaimed, and clapped.

"Can we have a minister bless our union?" Kayleigh asked.

"Yes, when he next comes to Caledonia," Graeme agreed.

"Will you make me wait until then?" Aiden asked.

"No." She reached to cup his dear face. "I love you and want you, my husband."

They kissed right there in front of everyone, shared a toast with whiskey, and went to the wedding feast at the dinner tables.

Their table was set with Aiden, Graeme, and Callan's grandmother's silver.

Roast beef claimed a place on every table with green beans, beets, and roasted potatoes with salt.

Dessert tables were full, with apple and pear turnovers, enough for everyone.

Jugs of ale were on the tables.

Rose had recruited girls from the village to help cook.

Songs were sung. There was music and dancing.

It was a day of joy to begin a lifetime of love.

Epilogue

Aiden leaned over to kiss Kayleigh, who held six-month-old golden-haired Micah. Two-year-old Rebecca, with her long black hair and blue eyes, sat between his bent legs. They sat under the kissing tree, feeding the squirrels. *What a beautiful family I have. Who would have thought it possible? Kayleigh's wit and my seriousness combine to make a unique life. I'm content. I remember a time I wouldn't have thought it possible.*

Kayleigh tilted her head and smiled, kissing him again. "What are you thinking?"

"I was thinking about how lucky I am to have such a wonderful family. We're blessed to have one another." He braided Rebecca's hair and tied it with a lavender ribbon, like her mother's.

"I thought maybe you were thinking about how intelligent the squirrels are." She giggled.

"It would have shocked you," said Aiden. "Our children are very intelligent. They've their own language, and Rebecca even speaks Micah's language."

"And thank goodness she does. She'll teach him our language too."

"She will. It won't be long."

"Did you hear them last night? She was singing to him, and he was humming with her."

"Mommy, kissy," said Rebecca. "Kissy, kissy." She puckered up for a kiss from her mother, who obliged.

"Oh, Rebecca, sweetie. I love you, dear. You too, Micah." Rebecca frowned, but she shook herself out of it. "Mommy kissy Micah," she said, and Kayleigh kissed

Micah with a loud smack. "Daddy, kissy Becca."

Aiden bent to kiss Becca. "Daddy, no kissy Micah."

"Daddy kisses Becca and Micah."

"No." She shook her head.

"Please?" Aiden asked.

"Please? Okay," Becca said.

Aiden leaned across Kayleigh and nearly fell on her to kiss Micah.

"Ooh, Daddy baby too. Mommy's baby," Becca laughed.

"Becca and Micah are Mommy's babies," Kayleigh said.

"Yes. Daddy fall on Mommy, Mommy's baby. Funny. Ha! Ha!" Becca laughed again.

"Oh dear, it was a joke. Becca is funny," Kayleigh reached to stroke her hair.

"Yes. Becca funny. Becca fun. Micah loves Becca."

"Mommy and Daddy love Becca and Micah," Aiden tried to be stern, and failed miserably.

"Hmph," Becca said, arms crossed over her chest.

"She sounds like you when you disagree with me," he said.

"You're right," Kayleigh agreed.

"Let's go home," Aiden said.

Aiden placed Becca on his shoulders, and Kayleigh carried Micah.

"Do you want to patrol in the morning?" Aiden asked.

"Auntie Brighde would love to sit with the children," Kayleigh said.

"Auntie Brighde. Yes!" Becca clapped her hands, causing Aiden to hold her legs firmly.

"I guess it's a yes," Aiden said. "Do you want to do

it?"

"I do. I would enjoy the exercise," Kaleigh said. "Let's sit with the children after dinner. Brighde can watch them tomorrow. She'll be thrilled."

"It'll be nice to patrol together." Aiden loved patrolling with his wife.

"We can have a snack under the kissing tree," she said.

"I was thinking of more than a snack break."

"You mean a meal?"

"A meal and romance with my wife, my heart, my love."

A word about the author...

Dee has a master's degree in education and a bachelor's degree in religious studies. She lives with her feline companions on the West Coast of Florida. Years ago, she excavated in Israel, and she bonded with a Golden Siberian Tiger. She loves family, cats of all sizes, reading, and writing.

Thank you for purchasing
this publication of The Wild Rose Press, Inc.

For questions or more information
contact us at
info@thewildrosepress.com.

The Wild Rose Press, Inc.
www.thewildrosepress.com

www.ingramcontent.com/pod-product-compliance
Lightning Source LLC
Chambersburg PA
CBHW060113260626
47160CB00005B/1877